A HEALTHY INTEREST IN THE LIVES OF OTHERS

Teresa Carmody

Autofocus Books
Easton, Pennsylvania

Published by Autofocus Books
autofocusbooks.com

2nd edition

Autofiction / Literature
ISBN: 978-1-957392-34-9

Edited by: Ryan Rivas
Library of Congress Control Number: 2024943050

"Observing the niche difficulties of being a writer, the shortfalls of writing communities, the challenges of lesbian dating, and nonlinear journeys in processing trauma, *A Healthy Interest in the Lives of Others* is a rich literary novel."
—*Foreword Reviews*

"Stories within stories. Threads that start, stop and pick back up again. Intriguing characters and lots of gossip. Teresa Carmody's latest work of autofiction, *A Healthy Interest in the Lives of Others*, is profound and playful."
—*The Writing Disorder*

"As the fig tree needs the fig wasp, so it is that the formally dense, deeply intimate fictions of Teresa Carmody thrive on the invasion of essay, memoir, and even drawing through their branches. What satisfaction to see Marie, the protagonist of Carmody's first novel, shift, like Balzac's Lucien Chardon, from the provinces into a literary world previously only charted by Gilbert Sorrentino's *Imaginative Qualities of Actual Things*. Carmody's is a tree very full of figs."
—Jonathan Lethem

Praise for *A Healthy Interest in the Lives of Others*

"*A Healthy Interest in the Lives of Others* is a dynamic, inventive, and hilarious novel radically attuned to the delight and awkwardness of human interaction. With an unsparing eye and the dark humor of Can Xue and Jane Bowles, Teresa Carmody depicts the life of the writer's mind."
—Patrick Cottrell

"What is a world when writing is the drug? Dryly, refreshingly funny, Teresa Carmody's sentences act like acid droplets in this cheeky meditation where writing is both the poison and the cure."
—Pola Oloixarac

"Carmody's latest in their long-running exploration of a character named Marie is a playfully profound meditation on self and community that centers the outcasts (poets, artists, puppeteers, masseuses, adjuncts, caregivers, activists, nonhuman animals) of a materialist, segregated, medicalizing, and oppressive heteropatriarchy. By turns lyrical, processual, and metafictional, Carmody's writing embraces vignettes, sketches, and visions as part of a spiritual summoning of a 'future self, queer and fluid' in prose as beautifully tangled as our deepest selves. Carmody reminds us that books can and should be an intersubjective practice of freedom, a home for our silences and hungers."
—Urayoán Noel

"Teresa Carmody's *A Healthy Interest in the Lives of Others* is an astounding novel. With craft and precision, Carmody removes any veil separating the readers from their characters, allowing us to empathize with the love and violence, passion and community, questions and humor, which fill Marie's world and all those in her life."
—J K Chukwu

for my friends,
especially Prageeta & Mike

"Is it fun?" Mary asked.

"It's not for fun that we play it,
but because it's necessary to play it."

"All right," said Mary, "I'll play with you."

–Jane Bowles, *Two Serious Ladies*

Poets learn about feeling as children in our
native tongue, and the psycho-social strictures
and emotional biases of that language pass
over into how we think about feeling for the
rest of our lives.

–Audre Lorde, "A Burst of Light"

Marie
&
Monette

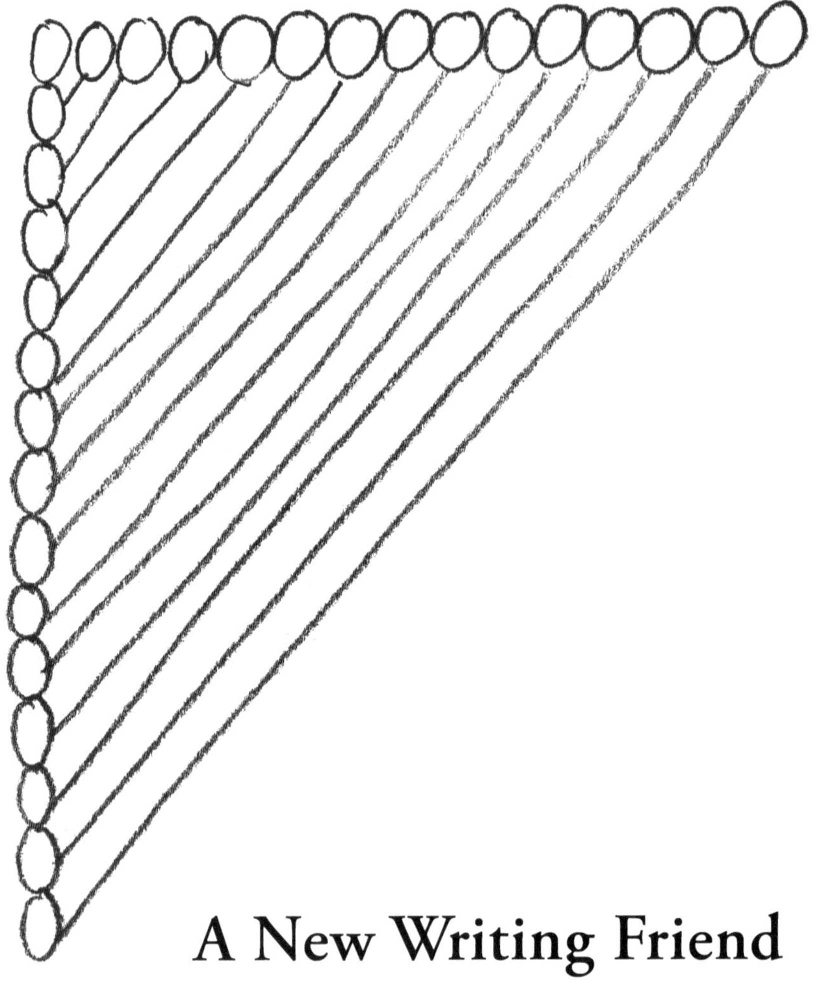

A New Writing Friend

a sentence makes a story

Because the two women wanted to change their lives, they enrolled in a writing class. All summer, they considered their lives as lived before and all summer they turned those lives into stories. The teacher, a thin-nosed woman with pale thinning hair, told the class, and thus the women, to avoid the new theory. It's enough to say the new genre, said the teacher with a little laugh, but the new theory will make you hurt. I like memoirs and monster movies, confessed Michele. Only my mother calls me Shelley, we love Frankenstein, but most canonical works bore me. I can't locate myself in books by dead white men, said Marie. It was a name she shared with the family dog. Marie had read some advice in an article for aspiring writers: Don't try to write The Great American Novel, the article warned. It will only clamp you up.

The California sky that summer was terrifically blue and the women named two blues to best describe it—true blue or deep sky blue. They often greeted each other by calling which of the blues best fit that day's sky. Our final summer of the millennium, they sometimes added, before entering the modern concrete building in Santa Monica, which hosted the evening course in creative nonfiction as part of the university's community enrichment program. After class, the sky became ochre, fuchsia, violet, midnight blue: colors on the flowering vines and trees around them. The women liked to name these colors, too, and their ability to easily agree was taken as a very good sign. Writers, they said, must learn to describe. Michele liked to write stories about old boyfriends and other people she had sexed. She had started sexing when she was fourteen, so by the time she was twenty-seven, she had been sexing for nearly half of her life. This math mattered to her, as did her shifting sense of what sexing might mean. What is your boyfriend like, asked Michele. He is industrious, said Marie, but he also drinks a lot of beer. Sometimes he passes out in the hallway or on the stairs and I must help him to bed. Marie paused. He would hate for you to know this.

Two years before enrolling in the summer writing class, both women suffered a personal loss from which they barely recovered. Michele had realized, with the help of a therapist, that her former relationship with an eighth grade Literature teacher was 100% abuse. She had known it was dangerous, that he could lose his job, she had kept it quiet; but the sexing began *after* she graduated from middle school and given the rest of her childhood, she sometimes laughed, she was used to being more grown than her age. Plus, he was the first person to encourage her writing; he said her sentences turned him on. Meanwhile, Marie had attended the funeral of her ex-best friend, Nina, where she met, for the first time in person, Nina's widowed father. The week before, Nina had driven her pick-up truck at a very high speed through a stop sign and into the side of a garbage truck. It was a country road; trees did not block the view. The police said it was an accident and Nina had, luckily, died on impact. Marie had been friends with Nina for several years and through as many psychotic breaks, during which

Nina would, eventually, be involuntarily admitted to a hospital by her emotionally-repressed-yet-well-meaning father. Nina said it was this same man, her father, who had driven her now-dead mother mad. Nina said her problem stemmed from sexism, not mental illness, and at first, Marie 100% agreed. It was a difficult friendship to maintain, and when Nina posted an ominous and slightly threatening note on Marie's apartment door, she severed the friendship. Three years later, Nina died.

Women are always wanting so much, Michele sometimes said, like their own lives and imaginations. This made Marie smile and want more writing. Together, they read a story about a Mexican teenager fleeing her US-American bully husband. In another story, a woman returned library books while her ex-husband trailed behind, complaining and blaming her for not inviting the Bertrams to dinner. They read about a girl who deftly completed the daily cooking and cleaning, though her mother said she'd still become the kind of woman a baker won't let near the bread. And then there was the story of a young black girl who found a man's lynched body while picking flowers in the forest. These were the stories the women chose, and the thin-nosed, copper-eyed teacher approved, as the stories did not seemingly include the new theory. There were other stories, too, selected by the teacher because they were true-to-life. The story of a colonial officer who shot an elephant and the story of a moth who danced and died uncomplainingly composed. In another story, a middle-aged white man watched a young woman with straw-colored hair as she rode around a circus ring on the back of a white horse, while the man mused about time and the authentic true beauty of original sources. Each story included vivid and poetic descriptions of scenes achingly full of significance.

Wanted, said Michele. I definitely wanted my Literature teacher though he was thirteen years older, and the first time we sexed, I was fifteen. She and her current boyfriend had recently adopted a grey striped tabby cat named Poe-Poe, and she was petting him as she spoke with Marie on the telephone. The two women had begun calling each other on days when the writing class did not meet, and they would ask: How is your story going? Have you decided to write about your Aunt Jean? Did you write about your high school boyfriend, Rickie, and if so, what did you call him? How did your Aunt Jean die? Will your boyfriend notice if you're not available for the next three nights? We must practice, said Michele, and she pushed Poe-Poe from her lap and began leafing through a glossy advice magazine for aspiring poets and writers.

To Marie, becoming a writer felt as likely as becoming a magician. Her dead friend Nina had frequently written stories, and Marie had once written a story about Nina, based on something Nina said. In the story, Nina was eleven years old and playing Marco Polo in the neighborhood swimming pool. She was It, eyes closed, moving toward their polos, when one of the teenage boys grabbed and pushed her swimsuit bottoms to the side. He used his thumb. His name was Tony. Marie gave a copy of the story to Nina, and later, during a tense period full of arguments, Nina spoke loudly into the telephone while Marie sat in another room, within earshot. I told her a boy did it, Nina laughed, and she believed me. She believes everything. Marie's forehead burned even as she suspected Nina was having a fake conversation, for as far as she knew, Marie was Nina's only friend.

Change, wrote Marie, is often resisted. One day, while the women stood outside smoking cigarettes and waiting for class to begin, the sky turned from their mutually agreed upon true blue to a striking slate grey. At this same moment, a yellow leaf fell from the tall oak tree in front of the building. The women watched in silence. This, said Michele, could be a significant moment. Did you see how the leaf moved slowly, back and forth, like a baby's cradle? She inhaled a deep puff and squinted her eyes. What decision do you need to make, asked Marie. Can you make your idea a reality? Marie looked at her cigarette and wished she didn't want to smoke it. She looked at Michele, who was standing tall and firmly footed. This is not my significant moment, said Michele. A significant moment defines you, if you believe significant moments exist. I liked the story of the moth, said Marie, but stories written by rich people make me angry. That's because you think their stories have more meaning, said Michele. In history, said Marie, they do. Why do you think our teacher hates the new theory? Creative writing, the teacher often said, relies on craft and concrete details. Neither Michele nor Marie had read the new theory, but they figured they already knew it, a way of perceiving the world.

Their final class that summer would be public reading of work written that term. Each student would have six to eight minutes to share, and the thin-nosed, small-boned teacher instructed them to consider their audience. Funny is a crowd-pleaser, said the teacher, and practice and time yourself as that is what professional writers do. The event would be at a small café that also sold clothing, bags, and other "indigenously crafted" objects from places like Guatemala and Thailand. Will your boyfriend come to our reading, asked Michele. Marie paused to consider. He likes his own stories best, said Marie, he isn't a very good listener. My boyfriend will be out of town, said Michele. What can we do with our writing besides publish it, asked Marie. I want to publish my writing, said Michele. I want to write a book about my old teacher. When people read it, I want them to feel the power of sexing, though I couldn't legally consent. Sometimes you're manipulated into wanting what he wants, said Michele. Before Nina died, said Marie, my boyfriend called her Your-Single-White-Female-Friend, because the one time they met, she wore my clothes and copied my hairstyle. She'd even mastered my laugh. Now, she doesn't exist. Will you read about her for our class performance, asked Michele. Marie shook her head, Not ready. Not yet.

Lives, said the thin-nosed, well-dressed teacher, are always worth living. Every life is full of stories, but not all stories are interesting to others. The key, said the teacher, is to make others care by writing stories with social significance and beautiful language. Don't whine, said the teacher, but let the reader feel your pain. This pain might lead you to engage in multiple affairs with young women half your age. Or perhaps you will need to care for your younger siblings because your parents are drinking, or working. Or dead. We have all been unlucky in love and money, said the teacher. We all know how upsetting it is when a stranger comes to town. Write something relatable. When I say your pain, I mean your character's. Perhaps your character doesn't know how to express his feelings, and this is painful for everyone, especially him. The lesson he learns will be even sweeter when he shares it with a reader. But don't make the lesson obvious. That is cliché.

They listened to the teacher and discussed her advice. I am trying to understand the deeper reasons I sexed my eighth grade Literature teacher, said Michele. I wanted to be stronger than my mother. Do stories always start at the beginning, asked Marie. The women were sitting in Michele's apartment and Poe-Poe sat with them, perched on the back of the couch just behind Marie's head. He periodically bit her hair and she liked the sensation this caused on her skull. That day, the women had declared the sky deep sky blue and they were drinking sweet red wine which made their lips even brighter. The story of my teacher is more than a story, said Michele. He was the first person who said I should write. I don't think my boyfriend likes my writing, said Marie. Michele nodded; her boyfriend listened to her every word. Are you writing about Nina, she asked. She wanted Marie to understand that boyfriends are easily threatened. The problem with my boyfriend, said Michele, is his fear of sex. He does not want to open to another. You painted your nails, said Marie. She grabbed Michele's hand for a better look. You should stay over, said Michele. Marie agreed.

Enrolled in the class was an older white man who often argued with the thin-nosed, clear-spoken teacher. He felt her both too relaxed and too rigid, though he wanted to make the most of this opportunity, his chance to write. He spoke about his feelings to Michele and Marie while the three stood smoking outside the building. It had been another true-blue sky day, and the man told the women he was not biased or unkind, but stories, he said, might only bear the appearance of truth. Consider, he sighed, the transitional object. The object is real and excessively real in the mind of the infant, even as it facilitates the space between me and not-me. Have you published any stories, said Michele. The man had, in fact, published a story in a local literary journal. You should send them a poem, said the man, for their "Leaves" issue. Our teacher has published in national magazines, said Michele. Why are you talking to us? The man said he liked their stories better than the others'. Sexy is a powerful feeling, said Marie. The man looked at Marie. What if, he asked, your Aunt Jean is actually gay? But she's the only one in the story, said Michele, who smiled and gave Marie a poke.

In class that evening, the thin-nosed, makeup-free teacher asked several students to practice reading their stories aloud. A young man with dark eyes read about his butterfly collection and the day he captured a Mission Blue. He realized, after it was dead, that the Mission Blue is a listed endangered species, so he was caught with a prize possession he could not show other collectors for fear of scorn or worse. Another man read a story about a father who drank and hit his children, including his youngest boy, a version of the writer, who hid in the woods where his father could not find him, his heart beat beating all the same. The teacher called on Michele to read her story. Red, said Michele. I see Rickie and I see red and I am on my hands and knees and he is behind me. Michele's story was angry and graphic; when she finished, the students burst into ringing applause. Are you happy with your story, said Marie. It was later and Marie was driving Michele home. It is a good story, said Michele. With good momentum. Though Rickie and I sexed like that only once. Mostly, I gave him blowjobs, she said. He called them delicious but also scary. Like me.

A few days before the public reading, the two women met to revise their stories. My Aunt Jean suffered a brain aneurysm, said Marie. But even before, she was weird. She was the only female in the family with a college degree, and she saved piles of newspapers. She wore blue jeans with flat red sneakers. Her hair was short; she never married; and every day, for almost five years, she called my younger brother to ask if the dishes were done. It was funny because he's a boy. Marie paused. But I don't know how to write about Nina. I didn't know, Michele sighed, that Rickie was sexing my friend, Sheila. It was after we broke up and Sheila began hanging out with skinheads. When I told her how I felt, she said I wasn't like the other Mexicans. I'm not Mexican, I told her, and that her gardener was probably from Honduras. Or El Salvador. Marie shook her head. After they passed Prop 187, Michele continued, Sheila wrote to apologize. She'd fallen in love with a skinhead; bad influence, she said. Did you really have an aunt named Jean, asked Michele. Don't tell, said Marie. Our teacher is rather fearful, said Michele. Is the Great American Novel always about white men and the women who sex them? Oh, Marie, said Michele. Don't be naïve.

Writing was becoming something more for both women. When Michele wrote, she used either a blue ballpoint or a purple gel, bringing the outside in and the inside out, while Poe-Poe sometimes batted her pen or sat on her paper. Marie found she could not focus if her boyfriend was home, so began spending long hours at a coffee shop. She also wrote by hand. Marie made a story called "Mind Over Matter" about a young woman who refused to mother her children. She made another story called "Hidden Forces at Work Are Challenged" that described a young girl who purposefully jumped into a river in the sky. Michele wrote a story called "Bright Prospects and Imagined Community."

It was so short it barely existed. In another story, Michele wrote about an older man who helped a young girl rearrange her dollhouse in a linear manner. It was a tragedy. When the arrangement was complete, the dolls were dead. She called this story "The Emperor Dominates Through Intelligence and Reason." This is the story Michele read for the class performance, and the older white man laughed at parts that weren't funny while Marie closed her eyes to better hear each word.

Class is dismissed, said the thin-nosed, bright-eyed teacher, with a wave of her cleanly trimmed hand. She stood in front of a greeting card display, proud that not one of her students had read over the time limit. The older white man clapped and whooped little cheers that did not catch on with the others. Thank you all for coming, said the teacher, into the already dispersing audience. In the final minute of the final day of the summer writing class, Marie turned toward Michele. Do you feel accomplished, Marie asked. Please, said the teacher, stay and drink more coffee. Buy some cards or beautiful paper, handmade in Thailand. Michele sighed and slipped her notebook into her bag, her newly revised story tucked between its pages. My boyfriend has left, she smiled. He won't return.

&

Marie and Monette peered over the dock's edge.

I'd rather be afraid than a fish, said Marie.

Monette spitdropped into the water. The plop radiated a widening circle, rimmed with light.

The lake was green and inky. In the distance, a patch of seaweed moved with the currents. Sometimes, and only in daylight, Marie and Monette stood in the slimy parts on purpose.

I'd rather be a bird, said Monette. I'd rather be a tiger.

Marie flushed. You always do that. Always is always.

Monette shrugged.

You must pick one of the two, or it's not a choice.

Monette squatted, touched the water. Why? she said. Why afraid?

I didn't say, said Marie. Bird or tiger?

Monette tugged off her nightshirt and rolled it into a log she placed at Marie's feet. Marie studied the shadowed shape, longer than her foot.

Marie grabbed, Monette pulled.

The water was cool and smooth.

&

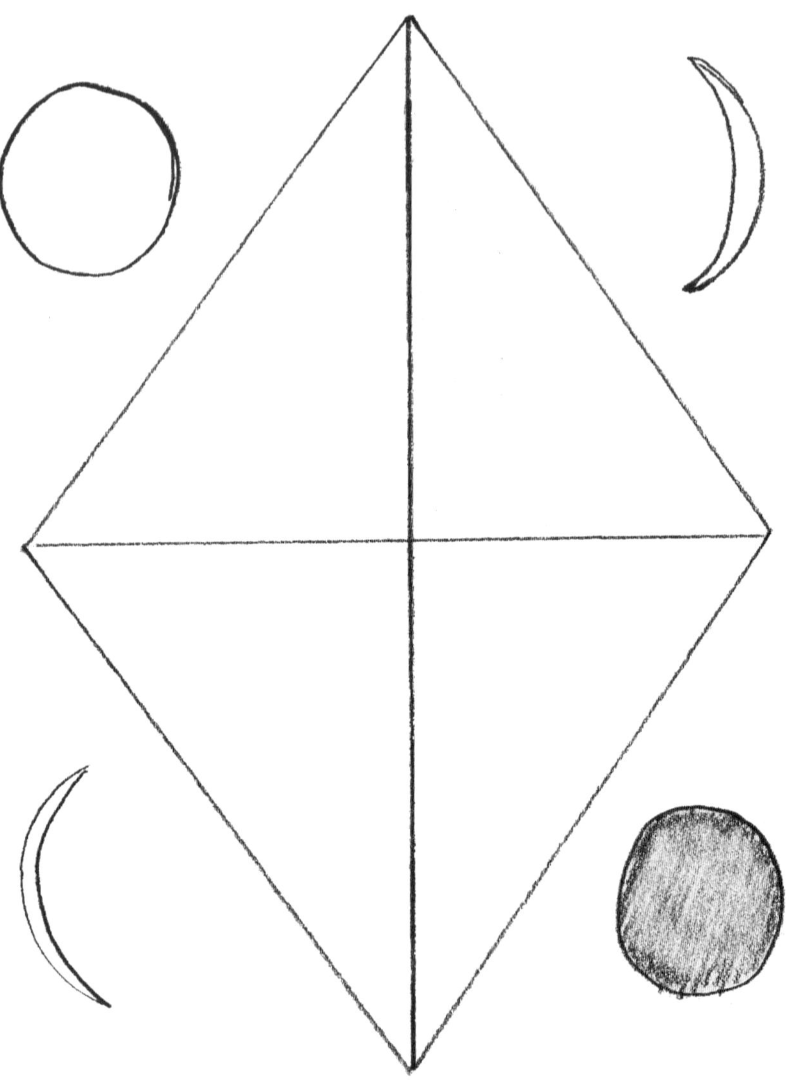

How Frederick Hides to See

portraits written in reflection, or the four of pentacles

Frederick knew there were parts of his sister he simply could not perceive. He did not share her experience of being female, a daughter. Or even a lesbian, which was different than Frederick's asexuality—how he identified as queer. Nor did he understand his sister's desire to turn her avocation as a healer into a salaried position, for such an act would necessarily shift one's relationship with Greater Purpose and hence, *the work. The work,* for Frederick, was writing. Screw the big five, Frederick once said. He brought out his first two books with small, hip independent publishers run by other writers who happened to be Frederick's friends. Like them, he wanted art unfettered by market expectations, though in the community, his books did quite well. He was seen as a serious writer, who sought to do something new in language, and he believed that, like the avant-garde writers he so admired, it would take only time, consistent effort, and a collection of special pamphlets— because who won't read a pamphlet?—before his writing, and that of his friends, would be heralded and more broadly recognized. And because Frederick was playing the long game, he used acid-free paper to publish his pamphlets. And because Frederick spoke of all writing as collaboration, he published pamphlets also written by his friends, their manifestos *and* feminestos. And because Frederick noticed the moon, not occasionally like his sister Jessica did, but nearly every night—Frederick knew himself to be magic. He could see into others, perceive their hidden motives and agendas, how they positioned themselves and wanted to be seen. Their backsides, which is a more accurate description than one might think.

Take Davis Burney, for example. In college, Davis played bass guitar in a punk band who put out an album with one of the hipper indie labels, which anyone who knew about these things knew was cool, and this was the 90s so "indie" was still underground. So much so that when young Davis told his most stylish aunt about his band and album during a holiday dinner, she laughed and said she had never heard of such things. In graduate school, Davis knew how and when to mention his label and album, especially while talking to girls and other subculture types. His offhand tone suggested confidential disclosure more than bragging—he was letting them see his youth, like how someone else might show an embarrassing school photo. Yet Frederick knew that Davis rarely played music now, if at all, and when Frederick asked about a second album, Davis admitted he was writing poetry instead. Frederick smiled understandingly. After Davis won a writing contest that included publication of his first book, Frederick smiled again as he read Davis' bio, which mentioned, in the present tense no less, both label and band. And when Davis' publisher hosted a book release party at a pop-up gallery in Chinatown, the editor referenced the band in his introduction and said he was looking forward to their next album, which—he had the inside word from Davis directly—was coming out, maybe even next year. But Davis was too easy an analysis, for while Frederick recognized his friend's legitimate talent, Davis wore his desire and insecurity right there, Frederick sometimes cooed, on his collar. Davis was like a waxing moon seen from the locked inside of an unlit fortress: the rock shone brighter given the absence of other lights, even as the fortress (in this case Davis) dimly relied upon one of the oldest and most basic lines of defense: looking larger than you are. That's why Davis punctuated his conversations with quick boasts, scoffs, and just-kiddings, and if he didn't have an easy or funny answer, he'd switch topics and begin talking about how awkward he felt when a barely famous writer complimented his work, or how his label keeps asking for his band's second album. But Davis' bandmates weren't at his book launch party and, as Frederick also noted, neither were Davis' parents or older brother, who lived quite literally down the street. Davis did, however, introduce Frederick to his trying-too-hard aunt, who exclaimed about the pop-up gallery and how Davey (as she called him) always managed to hook into the most happening things. But what would happen, wondered Frederick, if Davis simply said what he wanted? Does naming a desire make the risk more real?

Frederick's sister, Jessica, was his favorite case study of someone who refused to let things get better. Older than Frederick and wearing a habitual frown, Jessica often reminded Frederick that some people can't simply say what they want, and if they do, it may not matter. That's why it took her several years to come out of the closet (not to Frederick, of course, who already suspected). Her worries about not being accepted by the family were, in fact, warranted as each worry became quite true. Their older brother quit asking Jessica to babysit (he never thanked her anyway), and their mother, who blamed herself for what she called "Jessica's degeneracy," went through a heavy bout of drinking, in bed for weeks as their father said mother was having "a rough time." Yet their father continued to welcome Jessica to Sunday dinners, even asking her to arrive early, to help with the cooking, to make last-minute runs to the grocery for urgent yet missing items. He never wanted Frederick like that, and mother, who was critical of everyone, quit asking Jessica if or whom she was dating, but Jessica barely perceived this as relief. Thus, it was only a matter of time—Frederick had given her three months, or a change of season—before Jessica began to complain. How could she find her place in the world when she couldn't be seen at home? And according to Jessica, her work life wasn't better. She'd quit her first good office job because of a narcissistic supervisor full of backhanded compliments, and the next when she learned how much more her male colleagues were paid. (She had asked for, and been refused, a raise to the amount due.) She stayed on with the insurance company while she returned to school nights and weekends, earning her license in massage therapy, then almost-not-quite regretted the career switch when the only place hiring was a day spa that paid therapists only 25% of what they charged, far less than her salary as a claims adjustor. But she needed the experience and knew that healing was her calling, so took the job. That was eight years ago. Since then, she'd worked at nearly a dozen salons, and while everyone agreed she was a truly gifted masseuse—she had even begun freelancing and had classy-looking business cards and a portable massage table—her primary method for reaching new clients was still word of mouth and she couldn't, as she explained to Frederick, make others get the word out. (Sometimes clients worry you'll become too much in demand.) During those eight years, their mother had passed and their father, now retired, began avoiding the outdoors. Jessica met and moved in with Deborah, an English professor at a nearby community college, who accompanied Jessica to the now-infrequent family meals. (Their father still wouldn't eat Frederick's vegan macaroni salad—what's so great about mayonnaise?!) Frederick tried to remind his sister of her many positive changes, even as Jessica called herself a failure, said she was missing her soul's purpose as the world passed her by. On social media, she saw other therapists thriving, making videos, amassing followers, writing articles and sometimes books. Jessica wanted that! At least that's what she told Frederick, asking his advice on her website design, or if she should start a substack or newsletter. (What would she write about, Frederick wondered.) But he loved his sister and wanted her to live free of her illusions and the stuck-in-the-mud energy they produced. So, he told her to market herself with the same integrity she brought to her services. But as the years went by without much change, Frederick wondered if Jessica wanted sympathy more than success. She took too long to reply to emails and phone calls, and her critiques of others tended to conflate hyperbole with critical acclaim. (She didn't believe you could have one without the other; Frederick agreed, but just lightly.) In many ways, thought Frederick, Jessica was like a large tabby who, on the night of a new moon, wandered into a jail cell and decided she could not get out. The fact of slipping through the bars once did not mean she could necessarily slip through again. Meanwhile the cat grew fatter, making the bars work better and evermore. Yes, Jessica was a more complicated encounter than Davis.

Ana Falu was one of his more pleasurable engagements. They'd met at a reading hosted by their shared alma mater; Frederick was an invited author and Ana was almost done with a poetry MFA. During the reception afterwards, Frederick found himself standing with a small group of mostly awkward students, including a thin and slouching young man who kept vigorously inserting Herman Melville and Jacques Derrida into their conversation and a slightly older dark-haired woman who gently mocked everything the young man said. Frederick smiled at their collective anxiety, the endearing quality of their efforts and insecurities. A young woman also standing with them—short with thick-framed round glasses—watched the others without expression. Frederick noticed an ominous intensity in her eyes. She was full of being but not threatening, likely wounded though less likely to disclose how or when, even as she would certainly hold beliefs concerning why. The kind of emerging writer Frederick had learned to not ignore. When she said her name was Ana Falu, Frederick commented on its familiarity, and the older dark-haired woman laughed that Frederick must be hearing fate because quiet Ana would certainly gain acclaim and leave them all behind. A swan then, inferred Frederick, whose restful grace is as inevitable as the waning moon. He began to watch her at events and on social media, noting similarities and fewer discrepancies between "moon" and "woman," (though not, Frederick determined, in a female-essentializing way). When Ana Falu won a story contest less than a year after her graduation, Frederick was pleased to find it quite good. He had, by then, adopted Ana Falu as his private mentee, meaning that he sidled up to her at readings and parties and asked about her writing while offering indirect counsel. She was so obviously shy and timid about the gaze of others, and Frederick knew from experience that she'd have to surmount this fear if she wanted her writing to become well known. He also sensed her worry about a possible inner selfishness, so told her, at one point, about his views concerning a writer's duty to her readers. Refusing to read publicly, said Frederick, was one of the most ungenerous acts a writer could do. Ana Falu seemed to appreciate his advice. Yet with time, Ana Falu stretched the limits of even Frederick's generosity. On the one hand, he happily noticed her growing self-confidence, that she was publishing more frequently and her biographical statement had become increasingly focused, less abstruse. From a mutual friend, he learned about Ana's experiments with vibrational frequency and the natural world, and when he saw her at various literary readings and art events her face was brighter, her posture more secure. Then again, she still refused to give public readings and didn't seem to be working on a cohesive manuscript that might become a real book. When asked, she said she didn't care about the publishing gatekeepers, but Frederick couldn't imagine this to be 100% true. It was, however, an interesting avant-gardist strategy.

One of Frederick's friends said if desire were rational, it would not be desire; another friend insisted that shifting one's internal gaze changes what is seen. Yet Frederick felt that his calm observations of Ana and the others led him less to wonder and more to simply know. Many maturing people find themselves in this position, and the challenge, as Frederick liked to tell his closest friends, was not to resist the change but to step into the flow. With good faith, a true heart, and a clean conscience. Trust your magic, he beamed.

In that spirit, then, Frederick wrote a new pamphlet titled "Driving the Moon's Chariot: Harnessing the Power of Perception." In Part 1, he outlined his aesthetic philosophy for creative writing, which began like this: "We are doomed. Dead. Dirt beneath the soles of our children's feet. Dung excreted from our forebears, who have said and done everything beneath this blazing sun—condemned, we repeat them. Our only hope is to con vision anew, as hidden within the trap of language. Use. Different. Words. Put two unlikes together…" The pamphlet continued like this for another two pages, before Frederick allowed a break and outlined Part 2: Techniques for Achieving Greatness, with the tagline: *it's how you're seen, sucker.* "Embrace the force of the moon," he wrote, "which works in reflection toward its greater purpose. When speaking to others, elicit more information than you give; knowledge, correctly applied, produces powerful results. Use elliptical language, ripe with covert meaning, and if that fails, speak as softly as possible; the other person, concerned about mishearing, will lean in. If anyone is watching, they will wonder at what interesting thing you are saying. When you mumble even more, your listener may nod in agreement, and now you know something about their capacity for social pain and desire to fit in. And while you may see your friends and frenemies as competition, always refer to them as companions, never opponents, for every relationship can be mutually beneficial, especially if your companion believes that helping you was their idea, for which you are grateful (yes, cultivate gratitude). If you give people the option to help, they will choose to care for you and your writing, and you should help them in return, slightly, slightly, by publishing a pamphlet of their work; such reciprocity ensures mutual beneficence. If you help someone, physically and energetically, come into their own fruition, they can't blame you when things go wrong because your help was a gift. Light, as the moon knows, is best shown as reflection."

Frederick worked on this pamphlet secretly, thinking, as he wrote, about some writers with whom he was no longer friends. There was Joe from the record store he'd worked at when he was nineteen. Like Frederick, Joe was still writing poems. But Joe's poems were cheesy; there was no other way to say it. He didn't care for form and even, Frederick thought, for language, which is how he could write an ode to tofu, the upshot of which was, "oh tofu, how neat that you're not meat." Listeners would laugh and forget about it, while Frederick twitched and cringed. To think—at one point he and Joe believed they'd be the next Kerouac & Ginsburg. Hemingway & Fitzgerald. Wordsworth & Coleridge. No, that was when it began to break down, became too ahistorical, obviously romantic. Joe wanted poetry for everyone (and for everyone to like him), while Frederick knew that taking risks in your writing meant risking others' dislike. So, Frederick said goodbye to Joe, not verbally or actually, but with the same moral certainty he later used to end his friendship with Marie.

Frederick met Marie because of writing. She had moved to his home city and they began bumping into each other at events that featured strange and sometimes naughty writing. They both had a penchant for the weird, and for thinking and feeling deeply, and Frederick decided to help Marie, who really needed to learn the new theory, even as Marie began publishing other people's more exciting art. But friendships between writers can be, Frederick once said, notoriously dramatic, for any writer worth her weight is attuned to small shifts in affect, and writing is difficult and envy is as insidious as whiteness and the perceived authority of men. Every writer feels slighted and left out, unrecognized. But Marie, Frederick told another friend, increasingly viewed herself as a victim, which clouded her hearing. Her sight. At some point she quit listening to Frederick, quit agreeing with his advice. Thus, he wasn't surprised when Marie was trolled on social media, mostly for being married to a poet who defended predators while making increasingly problematic poems. Frederick saw the mocking posts but did not call or text her. What could he say? It was none of his business. Social media has its own binary logic, better to not rub her face in it and wait for her to call. He'd warned her about shifting times and tones, though Marie had refused to leave and failed to otherwise persuade her wife. Marie's love life was difficult for those who loved her. You have to understand what this is like for us, said Frederick. Such scrutiny and misperception! Having shared this with Marie, Frederick had done his due diligence and withdrew from the friendship, quietly and for good.

By the time Frederick finished writing his "Driving the Moon's Chariot" pamphlet, he felt vindicated in his friendships and resolved to follow his own advice. He would keep the moon to himself. For his next pamphlet, he would publish a fable, anti-fascist in its ambiguity and feeling. He would dedicate it to his sister and it would go like this: "The boy came to the barracks every evening. Every evening, he watched the light fade on rust-colored bricks and tall grass. He wanted to say something, but the words would not come.

He remembered a game he used to play with his cousin. On an outside corner, she would stand against one wall while he pressed himself against the other. In this way, they could feel but not see each other. Sometimes his cousin carried a goblet of water. They pressed themselves like leaves against the building. They took turns speaking and every story drifted from the corner. The boy knew it could not last. He ached and imagined her body already missing. When the wind blew from the east, he could not hear her voice. Later, he hid in a shadow. It was nighttime, the moon was full. Later, his cousin was angry. Later, his cousin stood too close to the road. It was the weather, the humidity, the hot sun. The air wouldn't move. He could sense her anger. Obscene anger. When she tried to blame him for the empty goblet, he knew he'd done nothing wrong. His glass was half full."

Frederick always smiled when he read this selection.

&

Monette showed Marie her shells. A pink one, a curved one, a clam, a snail, a shell for hearing the sea.

Marie touched the smooth inside of the curved shell.

Do you want a sixth shell for your birthday, asked Marie.

Only if the shell wants me, said Monette.

Let's play doctor. Marie lay very still on her back. The floor was clean and bare.

Monette lifted Marie's shirt and placed the clam shell on her stomach. She pressed her ear to its curve. Nothing, she said. She placed the shell on Marie's chest and closed her eyes. She hovered her fingertips above the shell. A planchette to Marie's Ouija.

What does it spell?

Not English, said Monette.

She moved the shell down, then further. Oh! said Monette. Such sounds!

But I hurt, said Marie.

Show me, Monette nodded.

Marie pointed at her knee. Monette licked.

&

A Healthy Interest in the Lives of Others, Part I

a panel presentation as participatory art

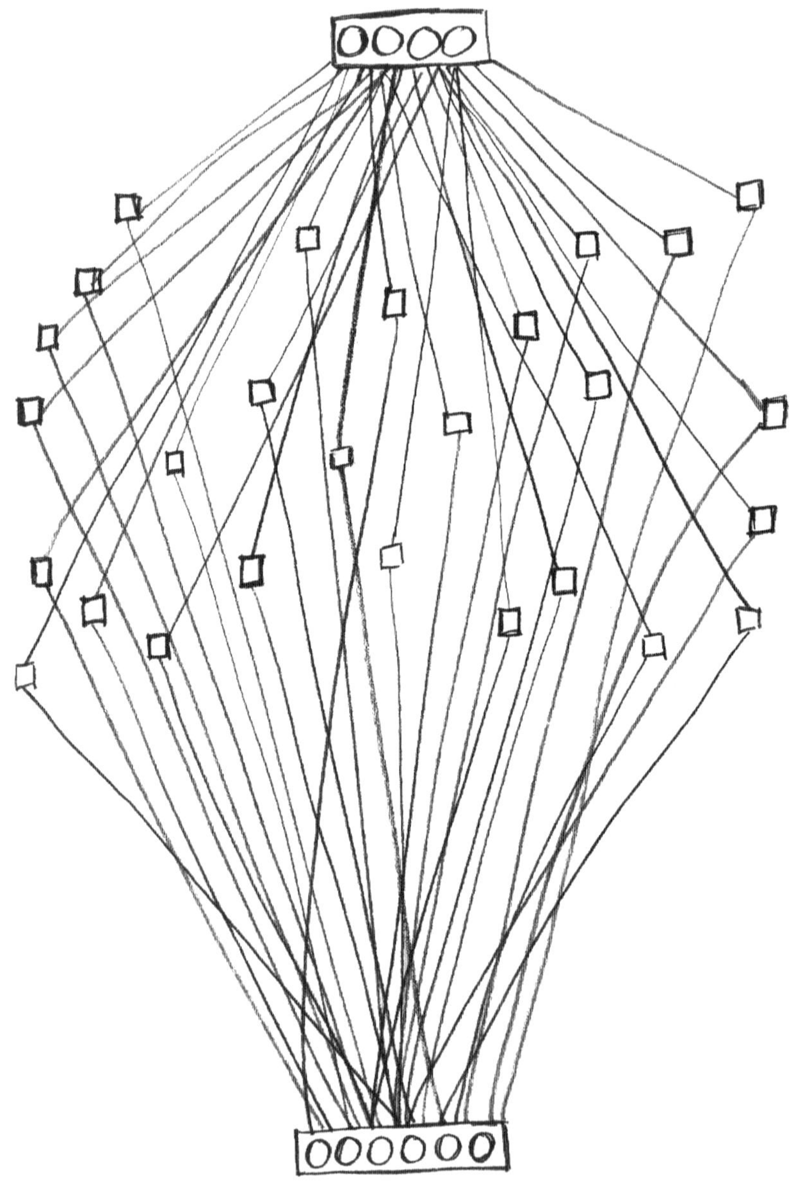

On another too-hot October day in Los Angeles, Marie and her friends gathered at a community arts gallery to talk about writing and publishing. They called the event *Be Papered*, a weekend literary festival named from a poem by Gertrude Stein and organized by a small group of experimental writers, many of whom were also editors and small press publishers with overlapping experiences and connections. Several attendees, for example, had regular exchanges with non-human animals: a lizard who appeared in a dream as the inciting image of a novel; a back porch aviary kept by an abusive stepfather as the base memory for a performance of bird oracles staged in a house that was also an art gallery; a small fluffy dog officially classified as an emotional support animal and unofficially held as a familiar who warned her highly empathic human of energetic toxins. Clearly, it was time for a conversation about interspecies communication. Marie was invited to speak on this animal panel, and while she had many experiences with nonhuman animals and frequently found them, cats especially, wandering into her writing, she did not want to speak, not yet, about the cats. Marie was in the process of moving on and knew this would likely be the last time she addressed this particular group, with its mix of estranged and cherished friends and writers she had, in some cases, published. She was moving to Florida, having accepted a tenure-track teaching position at a small private university, while her wife, Louise, was moving to New York, where she could work remotely and finally live her cosmopolitan dream; and because Marie wasn't, at that point, planning to end the marriage (Louise, she later realized, had her own plans), Marie directed her feelings of grief and loss toward her community instead. She wanted, if possible, to create a significant moment, one worthy of goodbye. She decided to use the Platonic ideal of a teaching evaluation as her model. She would gather valuable information to mindfully incorporate into the next chapter of her life, beginning with a guided group meditation and remarks about Socrates' recurring dream and how, in his final days, he began rewriting Aesop's fables as verse. She would conclude with five very short stories (anecdotes, really) about animals—two from Aesop and three from friends not in attendance—and she would pause meaningfully after each story to ask attendees: what *is* the animal's message? The audience could write their responses on the blank 3x5 notecards she would have already distributed, and which she would collect to incorporate their responses, their language, into a story such as this. She would, of course, give instructions for receiving credit (write your name) or a copy of the story (write your email) or for not participating at all (don't return the card).

Animal Message: *Non-relation isn't possible
(even non-response is a response).*

The event wouldn't start for another thirty minutes, but Angela already sat in the last row, waiting for change and doodling owl pictures in her notebook. It was a big deal for her to be there. One of the panelists—a poet-novelist who would likely speak either first or last because, like words in a sentence, those were the most memorable positions—was Angela's ex-best-friend. Angela didn't particularly want to see this ex-best-friend, but she refused to be defined by her and their broken relationship, which was a main reason she came to the event. After all, Angela was also a writer in the community and if she didn't go, how would she make new friends? She glanced around but didn't see any new-friend prospects, not yet. She looked at her owl picture, which suddenly seemed cartoonish. Is that how she wrote as well? Sometimes her husband accused her of this. She inhaled deeply and noticed which of her many mantras surfaced: *I am worthy of love.* Yes, thought Angela, not completely with feeling. *I-mean-I-am-already-loved.*

Angela wished to quit competing with her ex-best-friend, but there it was, the constant compare. Her ex-best-friend would probably always have more friends than Angela, for even though her ex-best-friend was somewhat reserved, she was one of those naturally popular people who exuded calmness and a solid-yet-appropriately-humble belief in their own genius, which, as Angela often noted, others sensed and enjoyed. It soothed them, like being the superhero's best friend—all warmth with little risk. Angela considered herself more intense and certainly more deter-mined than her ex-best-friend—the reason she'd become, in her quiet opinion, the better writer—and while she might never be the more popular of the two, she could certainly cultivate a better quality of best friend. She would rather have a few genuine friends than many superficial ones. The owl was quite good.

She heard a familiar sound and turned reflexively to see her ex-best-friend standing near the book table with two of the *Be Papered* organizers. Angela grimaced. Remembered to breathe.

Angela imagined her ex-best-friend apologizing for not answering Angela's calls or texts, knowing, as best friends do, that this icing-out was reminiscent of the neglect Angela experienced as a child. Angela wanted her ex-best-friend to say she was sorry, so sorry that she had misjudged Angela, had acted selfishly and stupidly, while Angela was not only right, but brilliant and irresistible, to which Angela would smile and say—*you do you*—before walking away, leaving her ex-best-friend with the same ache Angela felt in her chest, a hollowing hurt she would assuage with a new friend or two.

Animal Message: *My bond with you is beyond what nature can prove.*

Leon placed his bag on a metal folding chair and looked around the room, his chest slightly puffed. He was pleased that people were already showing up. A young man he didn't know slouched in front of a large bright kind-of-awful painting that hung on the gallery's east wall. He wants something, thought Leon, noticing how the young man glanced every few seconds toward the book table where Niki and Gina stood chatting with Ana and some woman Leon did not know. Angela, god he hadn't seen her in a while, sat nearby, writing in a large orange notebook, her body tense, dark hair covering her face. Leon tapped his pocket for his cigarettes, turning just as Angela saw him, so he pretended to miss her hello. He grabbed a bottle of water from the snack table before heading outside, to the far end of the gallery's parking lot. He didn't want the smoke to be a bother, though every time he "smoked on the edge," as he now called it, he felt annoyed for doing something of which Juli would approve. Juli, the self-appointed poetry queen. She allowed smoking at her house readings, but only near the compost bin that always stank of rot. Just imagine your poor lungs, she sometimes joked. Juli, queen of the critique was more like it, confusing that stick up her ass for being socially and politically aware. Leon smiled at her ridiculousness and blew a circle of smoke. She spoke at last year's *Be Papered*, which was why Niki and Gina agreed they didn't need to invite her this year, and Leon bet them a beer that, because she wasn't on a panel, she wouldn't show. Niki thought she'd come, but just to the second panel, while Gina refused to wager, on principle. Of the three *Be Papered* organizers, Gina was the only one who'd been personally invited to read at Juli's house. Well, Juli did care about poetry, Leon conceded. And she made some interesting poems.

Leon took a sip of water and nodded at his buddy, Frederick, who had just arrived. Frederick had been teasing Leon, in a lighthearted way, to take on a new anthology project that Frederick called *Experiment: West Coast*. Frederick made jazz hands every time he said this imagined title, a gesture that made the men smile. Frederick told Leon he was the best person to edit such a book, as he had the skills and connections, and a long-standing interest in the history of avant-garde movements and coteries, to make something *truly* representative. Something that mattered. But Leon didn't want to add such a tricky project to his list of problems. Because under the guise of bringing writers together, anthologies often made more enemies than friends, as the people who aren't included resent their exclusion while those gathered in the bouquet (the *anthos* of anthology roots to *flower*) believe they simply deserve as much, so barely bother to say thank you or hello. It was a matter of politics. Leon deeply cared about his politics, which is why there would be no anthology.

"Hey," said Leon, as he offered Frederick a cigarette.

Animal Message: *Communication is multiple, happens on different levels. Some connections are deeper than others.*

Cathy sat in the second row, beaming and wishing her panel was first instead of second. Her topic was fascinating—she had much to say about bringing poetry to unexpected places, though she considered it foolish to conflate publishing with writing. *You're the content, I'm the platform.* Cathy smiled at this sentence, the title of her talk. She'd been organizing literary readings for more than a decade, and last year she finally launched her own creative services agency, focused mostly on book promotion and general career advice. She was ready to go bigger, to start a speakers' bureau, and she wanted Gina on board—as a speaker but also for social media. Gina just might agree. After all, she'd invited Cathy to speak that day, proof that she was more open-minded than many other writers in the room.

Because it seemed to Cathy, and she wasn't making this up, that the more she worked with larger organizations, the more certain writers scorned or dismissed her as silly or l-i-t-e-lite. Museums and surf brands, transportation authorities and cosmetic companies—Cathy found they all wanted poetry in their programming or on their products, and she thought: what a great way for poets to get their work, their names, into the world. Cathy believed in community and liked the feeling of making things happen, but she was done with giving away her labor for free. Care support is labor too! Cathy smiled at this sentence. Her good friend William, another compulsive caregiver, had made her write it on a strip of paper she tucked inside her sunglasses case, so every time she switched spectacles, the sentence came into view. Cathy organized events because she genuinely enjoyed helping others. And: you must be the community you want to exist in the world. But as her events attracted a larger audience and more money, she felt how some writers—ones who didn't have much presence beyond their local friend group—began resenting her for not helping them in the same way. Oh, how Cathy couldn't stomach Entitlement. And its evil twin, Envy. After all, Cathy also wrote poetry; she'd just finished a series of apocalyptic villanelles that Gina had published as a chapbook. But Cathy didn't expect everyone, or anyone, really, to rush out and read her poems. At events such as *Be Papered*, she could feel how others wanted her to read and care about their writing, even as they stayed happily ignorant of hers.

Animal Message: *Friendship is only possible if one is weak and needy.*

Joel stepped into the gallery just as the first panelist finished her presentation, which felt right on time for Joel. He wasn't big on punctuality, especially for pretentious writers he'd barely heard of, like the first woman or the second, or even the fourth—who were these weirdos, and "be papered?" What the fuck did that mean? It's like they were certifying themselves as pure avant-breed dogs. Joel was there for the two writers whose names he did recognize, the two who wrote fiction, not poetry, which made them Joel's competition. He was new in town. He wanted to see if they were any good.

A doorless double-wide entry led from the smaller space in the front of the gallery to its larger main room, and at this threshold, Joel leaned against the entry's side wall. He took a sip of coffee. It was one of those giant to-go cups; he didn't notice his own slurp. His shirt was wrinkled, part of his look. Plus, he hated to iron. Before coming inside, he'd sat in his car, sweating, for nearly fifteen minutes, knowing the panel had started while eating a blueberry scone. He liked to eat in private, and not because his older brother used to beat him for being such a loud and gross chewer, who cared about his brother, he's dealt with that shit. Moved on. Joel hated people still stuck in their babyish wounds. No, he was a sensualist, who liked to eat alone so he could better focus on tastes and textures. The soft crumbles that melted on his tongue, the sudden squirts of sweetness and happy surges of sugar filling his cheeks. After, he liked to slowly examine his teeth, which he had done that morning in the rearview mirror. Then he checked Twitter. Before leaving the house, he'd posted *When people tell me they have papers for their "purebred pet," I tell them the Nazis kept a paper trail, too.* Fifteen likes, one retweet, two new followers. Not bad for a Saturday morning, and that much closer to meeting his monthly goal for new followers. He knew that social media was a dumb way to measure one's self-worth, but it honestly made him feel better to have people like or follow him. In the gallery, he resisted the urge to pull out his phone. He should have been speaking on that day's panel. He cared more about animals than most humans. When humans hurt an animal, he wanted to hurt the humans more. Someone tapped his shoulder, a woman with dark braids and big glasses. She gestured him away from the wall. Joel flushed. She pointed to an empty chair in the last row. He scowled and moved toward a spot in a middle row instead. It's not like a door frame is a wall used for hanging art. But whatever, he'd take a seat—see, he could play well with others. The woman speaking hid within her poofy hair. He'd heard of her, a poet-turned-memoirist, who droned about her attunement with extra-sensory vibrations. God she's the kind of person who thinks some humans are more evolved than others, and that dolphins and whales are the highest creatures of all. Maybe so, and she would place him, Joel knew, in the unevolved category. This pleased him.

Animal Message: *Patriarchy tricks us into attacking one another.*

From the front of the room, at the panelists' table, Marie leaned forward and studied the crowd. She knew her relentless self-criticism often morphed into judgmentalism, a weary and painful affair. Why couldn't she let others be? After all, events such as *Be Papered* were frequently the only public spaces where this group could talk earnestly about their admittedly heady and unconventional interests, like writing as telepathic transference and rhizomatic structures, or how living materials (bacteria, language) might co-create new scripts. These writers' imaginative wonderings became beacons within a world they wanted, a world that felt possible. Or maybe possible, thought Marie, because of course the world out there was also in here, and sometimes Marie wondered why she expected something different. The world out there valued some humans more than others, some languages or ways of knowing over other languages and ways of knowing. And counter-communities, like *Be Papered*, did the same. This was the kind of power dynamic Marie and her wife, Louise, loved to analyze and critique, even as Marie knew that some people, like Louise, needed to be seen as a Very Important Writer. You're more ambivalent about your writing, Louise once told Marie. Marie was not certain she agreed.

Marie caught Angela's eye and smiled hello.

But how difficult to connect with the poet who was speaking about her new memoir while tossing her head, like an agitated horse or wild pony, so her colorless long curls covered and uncovered her face. Marie was getting the side view, even as she was being watched, too, so Marie held her face in an expression of listening, nodding as the poet spoke with that slightly-pained-yet-sing-songy voice meant to signal lyric intensity. But that tone—really it was cliché! Maybe that's why Marie could hardly hear beyond it. The poet was using a lot of latinate words too, so many syllables to describe something she wanted outside of language. Marie wondered if the poet didn't trust her felt experiences, so must dress them in lots of sticky sound, around and around until there was a wall of words and not the open door, or portal, the poet called for. Writing, Marie told students, will reveal both conscious intentions and subconscious beliefs. Marie worried. What do my stories say about me?

Animal Message: *I don't possess the hubris to imagine what a nonhuman is communicating. The only animal in this story that is "saying" something is the human author, who ventriloquizes nonhuman animals to his/her/their needs.*

The poet began chanting words that humans use when grouping nonhuman animals: a shrewdness of apes; a congregation of alligators; a cauldron of bats; a sloth or sleuth of bears; a gang or an obstinacy of buffalo; a clowder, clutter, pounce, dout, nuisance, glorying, or a glare of cats; an army of caterpillars; a caravan of camels; a coalition of cheetahs; a murder of crows; a cowardice of dogs; a pod of dolphins; a convocation of eagles; a parade of elephants; a business of ferrets; an army of frogs; a tower of giraffes; a flamboyance of flamingos; a bloat or a thunder of hippopotamuses; a mess of iguanas; a smack of jellyfish; a troop or mob of kangaroos; a conspiracy of lemurs; a troop or barrel of monkeys; a blessing of narwhals; a romp, a family, or a raft of otters; a prickle of porcupines; a flock, covey, or bevy of quail; an unkindness of ravens; a colony or warren of rabbits; a crash of rhinoceroses; a cluster of spiders; a dray or scurry of squirrels; an ambush or streak of tigers; a rafter, gang, or posse of turkeys; a bouquet, confusion, fall, or wrench of uguisu; a venue of vultures; a wisdom of wombats; a school of x-ray tetras; a herd of yaks; a zeal of zebras. This is better poetry, wrote Marie.

Animal Message: *It's normal to have inexplicable preferences.*

&

Monette started it.

The girls sat in the middle of Monette's very own bedroom, facing each other at the small table with the blue legs and matching chairs. The walls were painted paperwhite with lilac trim.

Take a bite, said Monette. She bit into her peanut butter sandwich.

Take a drink, said Monette. She sipped from a plastic cup with a picture of a bear on it.

Take a bite, said the girls in unison. They bit their sandwiches and smiled at each other.

Take a drink, they said. On Marie's cup was an elephant, big and pink.

Take a bite they said.

Take a drink they sipped.

Back and forth and forth and back until even the words were empty.

&

Angela Writes Herself a Wife

a five paragraph essay that repeats three times

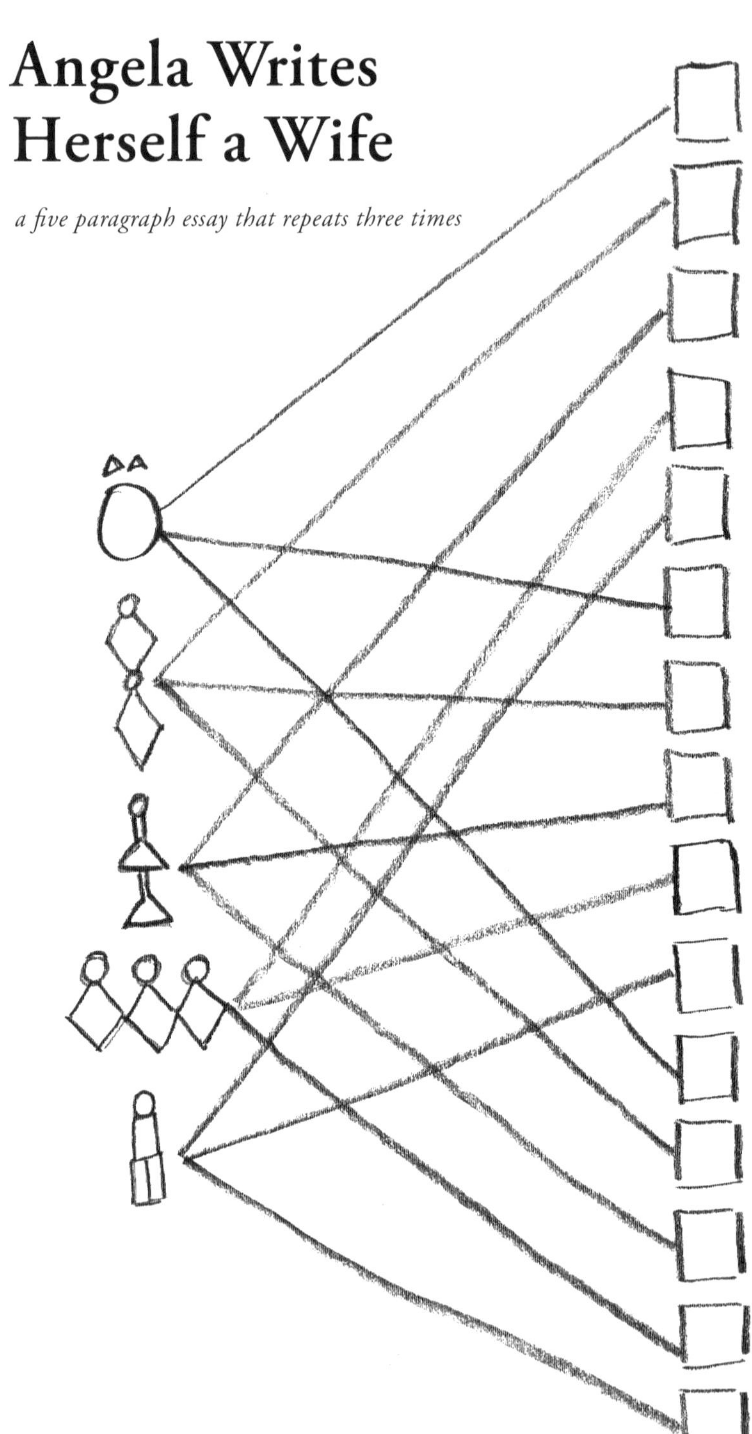

Mister Pants rubs against Angela and runs to the front door as Angela follows. Later, Mister Pants sings outside the window of Angela's soon-to-be husband's study until the soon-to-be husband opens the back door and lets Mister Pants back in. This pattern repeats, sometimes five times an hour, which irritates Angela's soon-to-be husband. He doesn't like the way Angela speaks to Mister Pants either. Loud and high-pitched, she frightens the creature, who hides beneath the soon-to-be husband's desk. Eventually, Mister Pants begins batting the soon-to-be husband's toes, and this, too, disturbs him.

Angela works in an after-school program earning fifteen dollars an hour. This isn't a very good wage, given her advanced degrees, but more than money, Angela wants time to write and she's practicing material contentment. When she was nineteen, she worked too many hours as a waitress at a restaurant famous for its pancakes. She found it difficult to stay focused and was fired after one year. Later, she worked as a hotel maid, making beds, cleaning bathrooms, and gossiping with the other maids in the laundry room. The hotel required harsh cleaning chemicals and after three years and three annual pay increases, Angela developed a sudden rash on her neck and torso. She quit by not arriving at her next scheduled shift. She has become quite health-conscious and prefers to help children with their reading. After the children close their books, she asks them questions about the story and the room where they sit. The children surprise her every day with mix-ups. Like how the puppy in the story hides in the classroom cabinet, and it might as well be raining in real life, the children feel so damp and alone. She is supposed to help the children turn their answers into five-paragraph essays, but she prefers stories to arguments. They're such sweet liars, she often sighs, how they tumble into truth!

Angela's soon-to-be father-in-law is a prominent family physician, a partner in a private practice that offers homeopathic therapies and acupuncture alongside let's-stop-the-symptoms Western treatments. Her soon-to-be father-in-law's father was a pediatrician, who left medicine for a distinguished post in the newly formed Department of Health and Human Services. A different era of Republican, her soon-to-be mother-in-law explains. Her soon-to-be husband's mother also comes from a prominent family and does not understand why her eldest child and only son moved out West, refusing his father's footsteps. The soon-to-be husband earns money as a freelance graphic designer and copyeditor, a temporary situation, he sometimes reminds his mother, for in truth he is a documentary filmmaker, actively developing several projects while cultivating industry connections. He wants to make a film about land use, money, and outsider art—think Salvation Mountain and Watts Towers—and is working on a pitch trailer, if only he can get it right. "Something will happen," he often tells Angela, who laughs because his films are mostly long shots of even slower action.

Angela and her soon-to-be husband are known to bicker. They have strong opinions about food and are suspicious of each other's allergies. Angela prefers plain meals of one whole grain and a dark green leafy vegetable. The soon-to-be husband laughs at Angela's simplicity, and buys a bread machine, so they can bake whole-wheat loaves to complement his Sunday stews. But Angela avoids gluten, and her soon-to-be husband's stews are slow-cooked, meaty, and full of spice. Angela tells her friends that her soon-to-be husband enjoys cooking, but when the friends visit, the soon-to-be-husband complains about their boring meals. He notes that Angela only works for two- or four-hour shifts, and he loves it that she's a writer, but does she need more leisure time than Mister Pants. "My soon-to-be husband," says Angela, "thinks he works like a dog, but he spends over an hour a day with his plants."

On the day before the wedding, Angela waits on a bench inside the airport. She is fidgety, for although the wedding plans are smoothly unfolding, she wants to prepare herself by soaking in a salt and herb bath, rather than waiting for her father, who insists that she park the car and meet him at baggage claim. Angela arrived early; the plane is late. Her father will neither ride with strangers nor drive in unfamiliar cities, and of course the wedding would not be complete without him, so here she is, waiting alone. She takes out a notebook and decides to write a love story for her soon-to-be husband. She titles the piece "A Great Deal of Contemporary Fiction." She begins to write:

Mister Pants is a tuxedo cat who likes the outdoors, and the bride lets him go, repeatedly, knowing that Mister Pants will only annoy her soon-to-be husband by meowing nearby. Before becoming Mister Pants, the bride named the cat

Arthur, and the cat lived in her small, ground-level apartment near the park. Such a smart creature, the bride often bragged, he did not need a litter box, the way he came and went through the bathroom window, always left ajar. So unsafe, said the soon-to-be husband, who tried not to stare at the bride. In those days, the soon-to-be husband was known as Boyfriend, and Arthur often sat on the bedside table to watch the bride and Boyfriend who liked to make good use of all four corners of the bed. After the engagement, the soon-to-be husband began calling Arthur "Mister Pants," and while the bride prefers Arthur, Mister Pants now hides when she calls this name, but comes running when she makes sex sounds, even if, laughs the soon-to-be husband, we aren't in bed.

The bride helps children learn to read and write, and most of these children live with only one parent and not enough money. The bride finds this work much more rewarding than her previous job of serving specialty pancakes to children who sat in booths with two parents and a brother or sister and maybe a baby, and the parents spoke to the children but rarely to each other and when they ordered, they did not look into the bride's eyes. The restaurant offered unlimited refills of chocolate milk and chocolate chip pancakes with flavored syrups and whipped cream. The bride worried that sugar was ruining American children, so began refilling "regular" syrup containers with sugar-free and forgetting the whipped cream and never bringing that third glass of chocolate milk. After the bride was fired, she worked as a hotel maid where she saw parents rent rooms without their children or even their children's other mother-father, and she lamented the loss and decided to abstain from having children of her own. It was a fancy hotel, but some parent-guests stayed for only a few hours and left sheets spotted with fluids, even urine. The bride's sense of smell is stronger than her attachment to the institution of marriage, but sometimes she still imagines the parent-guests pretending faithfulness in front of their children, and this upsets her: the way children are taught to lie.

The soon-to-be husband admires his very busy father, who works long hours helping sick children and ailing mothers. When he was young, the soon-to-be husband spent summer afternoons at his father's office, where he often sat next to the receptionist, drawing pictures of talking plants and the Chinese herbs prescribed by the acupuncturist. Sometimes, the soon-to-be husband peeked into the small rooms where acupuncture patients slept covered in small needles. The rooms were always dim, and watching a patient breathe on the table—eyes closed, pant legs rolled above the knee, white-tipped needles poking from the tops of his feet and in between the eyes—filled the husband with gleeful terror. Such change amidst such stillness: that's the feeling the soon-to-be husband wants to create in films. He knows he is a disappointment to his mother, who frequently ignores him. His mother rarely speaks to his father either, though she dutifully cooks his meals. His mother positively does not like the bride.

The soon-to-be husband recently quit smoking, so the bride bickers with him about other smaller matters. She doesn't like the way his friends stay so late at the house. Or the way his friends look at the bride, with insincere grins and appraising eyes. The bride does not tell her soon-to-be husband about the friend who said she could do better—the soon-to-be husband is already jealous and insecure! Instead, she asks what he and his friends do in the basement, aside from playing video games and watching movies on the over-stuffed couch. The soon-to-be husband shrugs. "We talk," he says. "About what," the bride asks. "Nothing," says the soon-to-be husband. The basement is the one room he kept to himself when the bride moved in three years prior, and while she's made some improvements throughout—fresh yellow paint in the kitchen, a new green and blue quilted bedspread—he wishes she cared more about the homemaking arts. He often asks her: "Don't you want our life to be nice?"

On the day before the wedding, the bride drives to the airport to fetch her father. He will stay at the downtown Omni Hotel, where the rooms are clean and tastefully decorated; these details matter to her father as he fears germs, bad paintings, and the color beige. He was hesitant, or rather, he refused to make the reservation until she went to the hotel and asked the manager to show her a room. Her soon-to-be husband says the bride's father is too demanding, that she should refuse his strange requests if only to see what he will do. But the bride doesn't feel like testing her father; she prefers to accept his phobias as positive opportunities to work through her own selfish tendencies, the result of being an only child. She wants to explain this in a fiction dedicated to her soon-to-be husband. She'll call it "My Monster: A Memoir." She finds a notebook in her shoulder bag and begins to write:

Mister Pants meows by the front door while Angela refuses to notice. Mister Pants has been at the neighbor's again, the white Spanish-style house with black trim on the other side of the street. Two men live there, a couple, Angela is sure, though they call themselves "roommates." Why? At this point in time, who hasn't had gay sex at least once in their life? Personally, Angela enjoyed it. The men keep feeding Mister Pants even though Angela specifically asked them to stop, and the short man with the trimmed beard and big eyes promised they would. But Angela can peek into their side porch from her upstairs window, and every day she watches the taller man put out a shiny blue dish they bought for Max—their name for him, not Mister Pants or Arthur, Art for short, as Angela also told them. Why blue?! If they paid attention, they would have noticed that Mister Artsy Pants's collar is orange, not blue, because that's his favorite color. Burnt sienna, to be exact. Last night, Angela's soon-to-be husband rushed to the neighbor's house and grabbed Mister Pants from the porch as the shorter man opened the door with a look of fright. The soon-to-be-husband threatened to report the cat as stolen, and the taller man accused the soon-to-be husband of trespassing. "That's ridiculous," said Angela, who pet the recovered cat for over an hour while telling him he was a very bad angel baby so cute so bad little baby so loved furry baby no no sweetie baby stay squeezed right there baby angel kitty on her lap.

Angela is having a difficult time as an after-school tutor. She doesn't believe in the five-paragraph essay as a form with purpose outside the classroom, and when the children ask questions her mind empties as she stares out the window at a rose gum tree, its pale bark and thin green leaves. She cannot help these children, they're so distracted; they begin to avoid her. The other day, she heard a boy say "weird-o" and knew he was referring to her. Her soon-to-be husband would like to be a father. He wishes she made more money and had health insurance. He often talks about more successful people who work in marketing or communications—better jobs than the one she has. When Angela's friends visit, the soon-to-be-husband asks them if Angela lacks ambition. The friends shrug. Angela says she is revising her resume. She has opened the document on her computer, so doesn't consider this to be a lie.

The soon-to-be husband's mother telephones the day before the wedding. She rarely calls and her voice pricks his ears. She asks if everything is ready and announces that she will gift the bride two family heirlooms, a bracelet and matching choker. The soon-to-be husband flushes and thanks her and internally credits this sudden generosity to his father, a liberal thinker and hard-working doctor, who insisted on paying the rental fee for the gardens at the University Special Collections, where the bride and soon-to-be-husband will have a small ceremony followed by a larger reception, surrounded, he hopes, by roses and honeybees. The soon-to-be husband looks forward to introducing his father to his friends. On the telephone, his mother pauses. Unfortunately, something has come up at his father's practice; tomorrow evening, the day of the wedding, his father will need to be on call. The soon-to-be husband's parents live one hundred miles away, too far to quickly drive in case of an emergency. They will be there for the ceremony and photos; she hopes her dear son understands.

The bride's friends wonder about the couple's bickering. "Angela is very open to others," says one friend, "that is her great quality." "I have never heard them bicker," says the second friend, "but I have heard about the bickering, the way he nags her to find a new job." "They must like to bicker," says the third friend, "or they wouldn't be together." "Well," pauses the first, "she told me she doesn't care about marriage, but agreed to the wedding because that's what he wants." "She said he makes her feel secure," chimes the third. "She admitted he gets jealous." "She likes more than men; how will that work?" "Every time I visit, they bicker about the cat." "She wishes he called the cat Arthur." The third friend pauses. "With so much FIV in the neighborhood, why do they let the cat outside?" The friends shake their heads. "But wait," exclaims one, "Didn't she call the cat Mister Pants the other day?"

On the day before the wedding, Angela greets her father at the airport and drives him downtown to the Omni Hotel. He is tired and for the first time, she sees his hair as grey. He doesn't want the bellhop to touch his bags, so she carries his small suitcase while he carries the large one; in the mirrored elevator, they appear as thicker and thinner versions of the same. At the door to the hotel room, he uses a wet-nap to disinfect the door knob. Inside, he wipes down his suitcases as well. He opens the small suitcase and takes out a wrapped present. It is something just for her. Inside, she finds a notebook with a white cover spotted in black. Her dad remembers her favorite colors and that she is a writer. In her car in the hotel parking lot, she opens the notebook. She will write a story for her soon-to-be-husband. She titles it "Life Is a Cat Named Art" and begins to write:

On the day of the wedding, the sun cast a warm orange glow over the small crowd gathered in the library gardens, along with the roses, live oaks, and flowering jacarandas. The ceremony was short and sincere, if also standard. And as the commissioner declared the couple husband and wife, a flock of feral green parrots swooped into a tree behind them. The birds were loud, excited, difficult to see.

Eight pines lined the dirt driveway, four on each side.

Marie hid on the left, behind the second pine from the road. She thought of Monette in the house across the street, at the window, peeking.

Marie ran around the tree, faster than the chaser.

She panted and waited.

Marie ran across the driveway, almost tripping on the uneven gravel. The pines were deep green; their short thick needles sometimes hurt. Marie caught her breath. She leaned and looked for Monette. She counted one two three four, then skipped around the new pine, careful not to look in Monette's direction.

She did not hear Monette open the garage door.

Marie and Monette picked the third pine and stayed there until it was over. They had to say sorry and mean it. They had to kiss on the lips to make up. They had to agree on the rules and sometimes break them.

Work Friends, or the Elements of Fiction Make a Story Go Go

a list made from lists drawn into a story
patterned by chance or the algorithm of gender

Allegory: *(n) a short moral story*

It was 12:32 p.m. and the four women were waiting for Gene, their boss and the owner of G.L. Corp, to stop by the break area like he did most every day after lunch. "Girls," he often called. "Break's up!" But the women, "the girls," had decided to sit.

A decision made spontaneously, that's how it felt. Because it wasn't right, they all agreed, how Gene had fired Ruth that morning without considering her story or even weighing the marks written across her face. He must have seen her eye, must have guessed how it happened. Over the past two months, they'd all seen her husband, a short scowling man who waited for Ruth in the stairwell after work. But Gene was a husband, too; he probably believed in husbands, of leaving what they did alone.

"I say let's sit here," Charlene had suggested, "until he gives her another shot?" Charlene was a small woman with big curly hair and the ability to wear corduroy knickerbockers with a don't-fuck-with-me flair.

A delicious silence sent shivers to the back of Marie's neck, bare since she'd shaved her head two months earlier. If she put on a baseball cap, she could easily pass for her fifteen-year-old brother. "Let's do it," she said. She glanced from Charlene, across the table, to Deb, slowly nodding at the grey laminate top.

"Worth a try," said Deb, her voice low. She pulled a Swiss army knife from the front pocket of her brown and grey flannel before settling, more solidly, into her chair. The knife was shiny and new.

They paused again, waiting, Marie later realized, for Jackie, who sat by Charlene. Jackie: sporty mother of three nearly grown sons, dyed blonde hair, tightly permed and bobbed. Jackie: the only one with a college degree, though Marie was working on hers and Jackie had married right after graduation.

Jackie sighed, "Alright." She was the manager, the forewoman, as Marie sometimes teased. They needed her agreement. Otherwise, they probably would have returned to the packaging floor, thinking about Ruth and feeling bad until easier thoughts took over—what to make for dinner and did they need anything from the grocery store and what shows were on tv that night.

But with Jackie on board, Gene probably wouldn't fire them on the spot. Especially this late in the season. So, they sat. Listening for his office door. Waiting for him to notice.

Symbol: (n) *something visible that represents something invisible*

They sat in the break area—a balcony platform adjacent to Gene's office on the second floor of a large, sheet metal warehouse in the middle of nowhere Michigan, surrounded, that late in the year, by harvested cornfields, golden brown and wheat colored. Jackie, Charlene, Marie, Deb, and Ruth, when she was there, packaged fundraising orders, the kind that came from themed brochures of specialty items purchased to support a child's school club or youth group. The items were not inexpensive, especially in 1993, before NAFTA and other economic agreements began globalizing "cheap" labor. But G.L. Corp, and the brochure campaigns they offered, emphasized the good feeling of knowing that your apple-scented candle or box of milk chocolate-covered turtles would help purchase new uniforms for a niece's cheerleading squad or send the high school marching band to Pasadena California to play in the Rose Bowl.

Setting: *(n) the context and environment in which something is situated*

G.L. Corp shared this building with another business, a garment factory on the ground floor, so the break-room balcony sat above rows of clicking sewing machines and the shadowed figures of women who were always there, hunched over, making shirts or skirts or something similar. Charlene guessed they earned by the piece. Jackie thought they worked twelve-hour shifts. Charlene wondered if they were legal. Jackie shrugged and said, "Not my business." Marie and Deb watched Jackie and Charlene have some version of this conversation at least once a week. "It's fucked up," Marie sometimes added while Deb nodded. They never said so, but it was hard to not notice the forty or so downstairs women as "not-white," while the upstairs women considered themselves "average Americans," not "white." So, to the upstairs women, asking too many questions felt nosy or not nice, like meddling in something you didn't understand, including the lives of women who may or may not be migrants, who may or may not lose more than a job if too much came into view. Yet the white women did not want to "make assumptions"—something else they sometimes said and felt good about. What they didn't say: How most of them could afford to take this seasonal job earning $4.25 an hour, minimum wage at the time, because they had someone else to support them. Or, as in Deb's situation, other gigs doing things she loved: teaching art classes and making pottery, which she sold at roadside stands all summer. When the women upstairs felt bad about themselves or their situations, they sometimes looked over the balcony and pitied the women earning by the piece. "At least I'm not working a sewing machine," Charlene sometimes said. Pity ribboned with gratefulness, then, about their better situation, for which they sometimes felt shame. No, Marie later realized, we did not create this inequity or know how to change it, but we weren't innocent either. Our privilege fed us. Our whiteness made us gloat.

Culture: *(n) all the knowledge and values shared by a society*

Their workday ran from 9:30am to 3:30pm, four days a week, with one 30-minute lunch break as mandated by law and two 10-minute smoke breaks because all the women smoked. It was November-cold outside, wind and snow, so they smoked indoors, as many people did then, around the repurposed kitchen table with its assortment of unmatching chairs. Only Gene, the owner, did not smoke, though he didn't complain when the women did, so long as his wife Rose wasn't working that day. She used to fill in, Jackie had explained, when they were short-staffed. But now that Rose homeschooled all five children—who knows what nonsense they might learn at public school, Rose confessed—the other women only saw Rose, always with the children now, if they stopped by because Gene forgot something at home. "They're Jehovah Witnesses," Charlene sometimes added, with a meaningful look. "Just can't get over no birthdays," Jackie added every time they came up. Jackie had brought in one of her own box fans to prop in the corner of the break area, keep the air moving, disperse the stink, and they always closed the balcony door, so the smoke stayed out of the packaging area. They couldn't say as much for the floor below, but the ceilings were so tall, could the sewing women really smell their smoke? Gene made them wash their hands before touching the mostly cellophane-wrapped products, organized on rows of utility shelves in boxes numbered to match the order forms of their corresponding brochures. Rows of the ever popular "Winter Wonderland" and "Snackin' in the USA" stayed up all season, while rarely selected brochures, like "Popcornopolis" and "Spring Flowers," were a welcome break to the monotony of Christmas gift wrap and seasoned Chex mix.

Character: *(n) a property that defines the individual nature of something*

Staying at her parents' house while on leave from UC Santa Cruz, Marie was home that fall because of recent rememberings into her own life. She needed to retrieve a notebook from her high school boyfriend, the one who broke her heart though some part of her had known, even then, he wasn't worth it—insecure fuck that he was. Yes, she was still angry.

Too angry, because by the time their relationship ended, she had desperately wanted to leave but couldn't get out. Why not? What wasn't she seeing? She wanted the facts.

For this, she needed the notebook. It held letters she had written to him during a time she could not remember. She had wanted to save her virginity for marriage, but something happened with him one January night when they were both sixteen years old, and everything in her memory went blank until Easter, when their sex had become normal, sometimes nice.

But worth the risk of eternal damnation?

Marie had remembered the notebook during a feminist self-defense class she'd taken two years after moving to the West Coast. For six weeks, she learned how to project assertiveness, especially when walking alone at night, and which parts of the body were vulnerable, no matter the assailant's size. One evening, while kicking in the corners of boxes and shouting "no," Marie began seeing the high school boyfriend's face concealed within the corrugated cardboard. She pressed through a rising feeling of nausea and kicked more precisely, but his ghoulish face reappeared with every corner, refusing to boot. Back at the rental she shared with three other students, she began searching her teen journal for clues. But those months were missing. Written, she later recalled, in a different notebook, a red spiral one she had given to him.

Irony: *(n) incongruity between what is expected and what occurs*

"How often does Gene leave his office?" Marie glanced at the clock. 12:37 p.m.

Jackie shrugged, leaned back to cross her legs. She wore blue jeans with a pressed crease down their front and brown hiking boots that looked polished, certainly clean. "He usually keeps his office door open," she said. She brushed something from the inside of her thigh. "That way he can hear how fast we're calling numbers. You know how I sometimes say we need to finish an order by noon, no excuses…"

Charlene caught Marie's eye and Marie glanced at Deb, who was using the knife to scrape dirt, or more likely clay, from beneath her short, unpainted nails.

"I like your knife," said Marie.

"Cat gave it to me," said Deb. Cat was Deb's roommate, who sometimes made too much banana bread and sent in a loaf for the gals.

"Oh c'mon, girls," Jackie said. "He's not a bad boss."

"Then Ruth shouldn't be an issue," said Deb. She wiped the tip of the knife on her flannel before slipping the folded piece into her front pocket. "What, does Gene think we don't work hard enough?" She pulled a cigarette from the pack she'd left on the table.

"No, no, that's not Gene." Jackie shrugged again. "But Ruth isn't the most reliable…"

The other women gave her a sharp look.

"I mean, really… she calls in at least once a week."

"Well," said Charlene, "she's tight lipped, I'll give her that. Yesterday I was asking after her boys—didn't she tell you?" She glanced at Marie. "They had to take one to emergency, twisted ankle or something. But Ruth said they're fine, all good. Boys being boys."

"Oh, I swear my boys nearly killed each other with their roughhousing," said Jackie. "But the youngest finally made it to varsity, just this year."

"Football?" asked Marie.

Jackie nodded.

"Funny word," said Deb. "Roughhousing."

"Oh, my sister and I pounded each other," said Charlene.

"I'm glad I didn't have girls," said Jackie. "I used to scream like a banshee, even if my brother wasn't hitting me. It made him think twice, but I was such a brat!"

Flashback: *(n) a transition in a story to an earlier event or scene*

That morning, the women were pulling orders for a big "Tis the Season" campaign, permanently stored on the shelves closest to the heavy beige door leading out to the building's main staircase. Ruth had arrived over an hour late, and the women paused as she entered, noticing Ruth's ungloved hands, her tiny body buried in a dingy grey puffy coat that smelled thick of cigarettes, even to the women. The door closed with a loud click, startling Ruth. The long bangs hiding her face fell to the side, and they all saw it: red, purple, and blue bruising her left eye. A bright gash above her brow.

Ruth recovered by turning toward the wall, unzipping her jacket even as Jackie was already beside her, speaking softly into her left ear. Evidently, Gene had told Jackie to send Ruth in, when and if she showed up. Marie, Charlene, and Deb learned these details later, during the lunchtime talk that led to their staying put. Because who cared if Ruth hadn't called. She couldn't! Her phone didn't work!

The women didn't know this, though, when Ruth, still in her jacket, left Gene's office less than five minutes later, face buried in the grey puff as she pushed through the putty-colored door. "Wait," called Charlene, who tossed aside a Merry Mail Christmas Card holder and followed her out. Gene watched from his office doorway, breathing heavily, thumbs tucked in his front pockets.

"Jackie," he said. For a moment, his eyes rested on Marie.

Foil: *(v) hinder or prevent, as an effort, plan, or desire*

Was sex worth the risk of eternal damnation?

Not with boys, Marie would later realize.

Yet at this point in her life—twenty years old and working at the warehouse—Marie was honestly too scared to have sex, even if the fear came from Christian radio, a constant broadcast in her mother's kitchen. Marie didn't like those pastors, didn't agree with them or their politics, but she didn't like the panic attacks she was having either; the thought of sex always brought one on. She did not judge her friends for having sex, but for herself, she wanted more say. That's why she reclaimed her virginity, bought herself a purity ring, and refused to sleep with her current boyfriend, even after he became born again. And when she couldn't stop random catcalls on the street, and when someone said trauma got stuck in the hair, and when she saw other young women with beautiful, Sinead O'Connor, bald heads, she decided to shave hers and change her script. For she had also discovered feminism and marijuana and the Grateful Dead and Ani DiFranco and radical education, like Paulo Freire's *Pedagogy of the Oppressed*, and while she was thinking about proposing to her boyfriend when she returned to the West Coast—wasn't that the next logical step?—it also felt weird, maybe even wrong, for her to marry him.

Narrator: *(n) someone who tells a story*

Now the reader must be noticing that these elements of fiction are hardly the most "essential," and several carry awkward definitions, sometimes of another meaning held within that same word. Marie, of course, is narrating this story. Not the Marie who was twenty years old, closeted, and worried about sex, but Marie as her future self, queer and fluid, still prone to worry and wanting sex to be easy and fun, but intense and intimate, vulnerable but also pleasurable for the sake of pleasure, all surface, all depth. Which is what the future Marie also wants from writing. Paradox. Contradiction. Future Marie will sometimes write *woman* to mean a marginalized body, regardless of identity, and *story* for the variant ways a textual body in prose can take a shape, pattern, or form. "Woman," the future Marie will realize, is a word claimed and constructed, like a story, and what are the elements of fiction except tools to make a story go go. Future Marie consolidated several "Elements of Fiction" vocabulary lists, compiled by teachers around the United States and catalogued on vocabulary.com, before clicking on the website's quiz randomizer tool to select which elements would create this story, and because the teachers were probably tired, and likely underpaid, the list included words with definitions erroneously copied and pasted from other numbered meanings, which made some of these "Elements of Fiction" quite strange. Marie liked this.

Atmosphere: *(n) distinctive but intangible quality around a person or thing*

The women hated Gene's smirk. That's how the lunchtime conversation had started. His half smile and unmoving eyes. Jackie described how, walking into Gene's office after Ruth left, he gave step-by-step instructions for terminating her employment. As if Jackie hadn't been doing her job for the past five years! As if Ruth deserved it. And have you noticed how Rose, his wife, clams up whenever Gene's around? Marie had never worked with Rose, but Charlene swore that woman could talk your ear off, going on about teaching her eldest girls how to sew and can tomatoes and other wifely skills. No wonder Gene wanted her to homeschool their children, turn those girls into useful housebodies. She was probably good at it, too, so long as Gene wasn't home.

"Men disgust me," said Charlene. She tapped the list they'd been making with her pen. That morning, Charlene was surprised to see that Ruth had driven herself to work, though Charlene reached Ruth's car window just in time. When Ruth said her phone was disconnected, Charlene took her home address instead. The initial plan was to bring groceries that evening, but the more the women talked, the more they realized Ruth needed. "Potatoes, chicken, milk, butter, eggs, carrots, and pudding. Anything else?" When the other women shook their heads, Charlene folded the list, along with the five- and twenty-dollar bills they'd pooled for Ruth and the boys.

"What do you think those boys are learning," said Deb, "living in that home?"

Motif: *(n) a recurrent element in a literary or artistic work*

Usually, the lunchtime conversation was about Charlene, whose life was full of dramatic turns and way too much trauma. When Charlene was three, her mother disappeared into the who-knows-where, so Charlene and her younger sister grew up between creepy relatives and foster care. "It was what it was," Charlene said, and no, she had never known her father. Not until later, married with children of her own, when Charlene tracked him down. There were a few good years of getting to know him, even if he seemed somehow off. According to him, he hadn't known the girls were motherless, or he would've done something. Charlene didn't believe him, but her sister did and for the sake of her own children's relationship with grandpa, Charlene let it go. Until the day she found grandaddy doing she-won't-say-what to her eight-year-old daughter, Sarah. This time it was Charlene who called the State. But Charlene's sister refused to "lose Daddy," not again, so posted bail for him instead. "That was the final straw," said Charlene, who hadn't spoken to her sister since.

Quote: *(v) repeat a passage from*

"Women must write her self: must write about women and bring women to writing, from which they have been driven away as violently as from their bodies—for the same reasons, by the same law, with the same fatal goal."

–Hélène Cixous, "The Laugh of the Medusa"

Rhythm: *(n) an interval during which a recurring sequence occurs*

12:41 p.m. and still no sign of Gene.

"Anyway," said Deb, tapping the table with her index finger, "Ruth doesn't have to tell us her business. Do we want to help or not?"

"We're still sitting here, aren't we?" said Jackie.

Marie nodded. They could, she realized, change their minds. Like you could decide one thing, then reverse your decision. Even if it disappointed others. She pulled a hoodie from the backpack she'd shoved beneath her chair. The movement released a small stream of wetness between her legs. "Oh, shit," she said. The bloating made sense. "I think I just started bleeding. Does anyone have a pad?"

Deb rummaged through her purse.

"I know I don't," said Charlene. "Almost forgot my lunch this morning." They'd gotten the first snow of the season the night before and Charlene, who gave Marie rides to and from work, had been running late. "Had to scrape the ice off," she'd explained when Marie got in the car. "It's nice to smash something you're supposed to break."

Marie had laughed and hoped to be like Charlene one day: to speak as she felt.

Deb handed the light-yellow pouch to Marie. "Sorry," she said. "It's extra-long."

Jackie watched with an unfocused expression. "You know," she said to Deb, "Bill's never done anything like this."

"Like what?" said Marie. Jackie rarely spoke about her husband.

"Oh, you don't know," said Jackie, who began to slightly rock in her chair. "Bill's a supervisor at Steelcase," she explained. "He always teases that my job is a play version of his." She wiped the edge of her mouth. "But he's never done nothing like this."

"A sit-in?" said Deb. "Is that what this is called?"

"We're real revolutionaries," joked Charlene.

Marie laughed. Jackie nodded.

"I'm glad we're sitting," said Marie. Deciding again.

Tone: *(n) a quality that reveals the attitude of the author*

Charlene used a cushion to see over the steering wheel of her 1984 Dodge Raider. Marie began riding with her that first week, after Charlene stayed one day to chat with Jackie, and coming out of the building twenty minutes later, found Marie sitting on a parking curb near the main door. Marie had bicycled her first two days—a flat, easy four miles—but it had been raining that morning, so Marie's mom dropped her off. Maybe her mom would remember to pick her up, or maybe Marie should begin walking. When Charlene learned that Marie lived just off her usual route, she offered daily rides. Honestly, Marie loved them.

Charlene was older than Marie's elder sister, but fifteen years younger than Marie's parents, who did not understand why Marie was back in Michigan but still paying rent for a room in Santa Cruz. They wanted her to give up this "California thing," move back and, if she insisted on education, go to a Christian college at least. If Marie wanted California, she would have to pay for it; if she was living in their house, she would have to get a job. If she got a job, she would have to figure out transportation. They never asked Marie about the "stuff" she was home to deal with. If they had asked, Marie wouldn't have told them. When Marie arrived at the airport in early September, a black hoodie covering her shaved head, her mother said she only knew Marie because of her green Doc Martens.

Marie shared these details with Charlene over their fifteen-minute drives every morning and afternoon. "You've heard all about my screwed-up life," said Charlene, after Marie told her about the high school boyfriend. And later, about calling him and arranging a time to meet. Like old times, he did not have a car, so Marie borrowed her mother's and picked him up, and they went to the same Denny's everyone used to go to. He said Marie's shaved head scared him and Charlene said, "Ha!" He accused Marie of "talking smart" to make him feel bad, and Marie said, "I am smart," and Charlene said, "Good girl!" Yes, he had the notebook and would return it. But when Marie pulled into his driveway and told him to get it, he changed his mind. "It was a gift," he said. But Marie would sit there all night if she had to, she would make a madfuss like nothing he'd ever seen, she wasn't leaving without it. So what if the letters were to him. It was her writing. Hers. And she would not leave without it, they both knew.

Reading the notebook was unbearable. For what happened but also for who she had been: a teenage girl so hopelessly lonely and trained to blame herself for being "irrational and too emotional," for being "annoying" and "acting like a bitch." Week after week, she apologized and pled with her boyfriend to please not be angry. He would withdraw, disappear, he would accidently "forget about her." He made plans with other girls who were "just friends."

She became increasingly desperate.

She did not tell Charlene any of this. Nor the details she had not remembered. Like how it had been March, not January. How she had panicked. How just that day filled the whole second half of the notebook, even as she didn't have language for what occurred. She was afraid to name it. Her parents' telephone was not working that evening, so she had bicycled to a friend's house, then to another's, then two more miles to a gas station pay phone. Every time she called him, the boyfriend was out. "I feel dead," she wrote. "That wasn't sex," the boyfriend later argued. He wanted the "real" experience. "You are," she wrote, "the most special thing that ever happened to me."

Charlene glanced at Marie. "How are you?" she asked.

"Yes," she told Charlene. "The notebook confirmed it."

"I had a dream about you," said Charlene the following morning. "You published a fiction book."

"Oh!" said Marie.

Plot: *(n) a small area of ground covered by specific vegetation*

The restroom was on the other side of Gene's office, near the bin where they tossed empty boxes to be broken down at the end of each day. As she passed, Marie glanced at Gene's shadowed figure behind the thin white blinds—strange for him to stay in there so long after lunch, and with the door shut. Marie heard him laugh.

The restroom was stained beige tiles, an overflowing trash can, and, shoved behind the manufactured-wood door, a dirty mop with a bucket holding worn rubber gloves and half-used bottles of cleaning supplies. Marie arranged toilet paper over the toilet seat. She had made a bright-red blot in the lining of her cotton panties. She wiped her blood's surface and sniffed the toilet paper. She loved that penny metallic scent, her moon juice, as a friend in Santa Cruz called it, and smelled this close, it overpowered the old urine and chemical smell of the restroom. This blood, this vagina—that's why her dad wouldn't teach her about cars and why her mom worried she was selfish. Sure, there were hormones, chemicals, other physical differences, but these were elements up for revision. For reinterpretation. Because the cultural meaning attached to bodies—who gets perceived as meaningful, reliable, significant, worthy of being a one and only main character in a story hailed as perfect, masterful, genius, true art—were fictions, socially constructed. Even chance has a pattern, written on our bodies. And stories selected for commercial publication, Marie would learn, often maintained the status quo.

Conflict: *(n) a state of opposition between persons or ideas or interests*

Back in the break area, Marie found the others standing at the platform railing and watching the women below. There were forty or so stations, each with a small machine.

"It's worth asking," said Jackie with a sniff. She tapped her watch, then glanced at the clock on the breakroom wall. 12:47 p.m. "Weird," she said.

Marie slid into the space by Deb. "What's going on?" she asked.

Charlene leaned back to peer around Deb. "Jackie had the idea of asking their manager to hire Ruth," she said. "In case Gene says no."

"Do you think he will?" said Marie.

"I don't know what's taking him so long," said Jackie.

"If it's piece work," joked Charlene, "they might be open to Ruth missing a day or two…"

The other women sighed in Charlene's direction. "Look," continued Charlene, "everyone says to 'see the positive.' I know for certain she needs the work."

"Depending on how this goes down," shrugged Deb, "I might need a new job, too. Cat can't cover the mortgage alone."

"Doesn't Cat pay you rent?" asked Charlene.

"If he fires you all," said Jackie, "I'm going with you." Again, she glanced at her watch. "I can make shirts or whatever."

"It doesn't look like shirts to me," said Marie. "Do you really think he's going to fire us?"

"Nah," said Jackie.

"Is Cat on the house title?" asked Charlene.

"Skirts, maybe?" Deb leaned forward while tugging at the eyeglasses in her front pocket. Something fell. "Shit," said Deb.

Her pocketknife lay like a silver comma on the floor below, five feet or so from a woman in a white t-shirt with short dark hair. The woman noticed the knife before looking at the women upstairs. On her shirt, Mickey Mouse ran in yellow shoes beneath three red and blue letters: USA.

"Sorry about that," shouted Charlene. Marie waved. Deb had already left the break area.

"She's coming to get it," called Charlene.

Marie and Charlene followed the downstairs woman's glance toward the other side of the room. An office, not unlike Gene's, with glass windows and a glass-paned door, closed, like Gene's door, though the blinds were up. A figure lurked.

Downstairs, the dark-haired woman moved in a quick motion, ducking to snatch the pocketknife, which she tucked into the waistband of her jeans before slipping back into her seat, same spot, same direction. She said something into the machine—*after, laughter, later*—hard to hear given the clicking and whirring all around. Palms down, she made two quick x's and pointed toward the office.

The figure behind the window moved.

"Fuck," said Charlene who took off after Deb. Marie ducked. Jackie turned around.

"I'm going to talk to him," Jackie said.

Tension: *(n) a balance between opposing elements or tendencies*

By the time Deb and Charlene came up the main staircase, Marie was waiting in the packaging area, just on the other side of the beige door. Jackie was still in Gene's office. Marie had lined up four cardboard boxes, empty side down, outside of Gene's immediate view.

"But handkerchiefs?" said Deb.

"I had to come up with something," said Charlene.

Marie gestured quiet and nodded toward Gene's door. "C'mon," she said, coaxing the other women toward the boxes. "What happened?" she asked.

"I have never smelt a man so covered in liver and onions," whispered Deb. She shook her head. "The door was locked and by the time that smelly little man showed up—I did not like his vibe, not a bit—Charlene was there exclaiming about my handkerchief… my snot rag… saying she found it under the chair."

"I couldn't think beyond a lost object," interrupted Charlene, "but when Deb didn't get it, I just switched stories and started telling him that Deb makes her own handkerchiefs, they're real pretty, pink and green, but his face was blank, even those beady blue eyes. I said, 'Do you have any applications, sir?' Well, that woke him up. He wanted to know how I knew about the factory, and I said we worked upstairs, but the season would be ending."

"Handkerchiefs?" whispered Marie.

"Exactly," said Deb. She rolled her eyes in pleasure.

"Look," said Charlene, "sometimes you got to make shit up." She elbowed Marie. "That's fiction," she said.

"Oh, he didn't believe us," laughed Deb. "But he couldn't figure out what we wanted."

"He said come back when we're done for the season, he'll see what he has." Charlene snorted.

"But that irritated me," said Deb. "Why doesn't he have applications? So, I said 'Surely you have them. Please, sir,' I said. And boy did that aggravate him. 'I don't have time for this,' he said, and he pulled the door shut, right in our faces."

"Smelly little small-handed man," said Charlene. "Did you see his hands?"

Deb nodded.

"At least we didn't get that worker in trouble," said Charlene.

"Yeah," said Deb. She paused. "So… I guess I'll wait for the end of her shift."

The silence that followed gave space for absorption. There was so much Marie did not understand.

Charlene looked at the boxes. "What's this?" she asked.

"Did I ever tell you about my self-defense class?" Marie shifted the box closest to her, just like she wanted. "Imagine that corner as a knee cap." Positioning herself adjacent to the cardboard, she balled her fists, arms drawn closely in.

Gene's door opened. The women took in Jackie's face, blank and unblinking. "Back to work," Jackie said.

Marie kicked anyway, the vertex crumpling into the empty inside before anyone could say no.

They make me feel small, sighed Marie.

Not me, said Monette. They're my cousins.

Really?

Monette smiled and stretched back even further. Do you want me to flip?

Don't you mean "like" your cousins?

Monette landed on her open palms, belly bridging toward the sky.

To be "like" something isn't the same as being something.

Watch, said Monette. She kicked her legs up, one then another. Your turn, she said.

Marie checked the ground for night bugs. She didn't see any, but that didn't mean they weren't there.

Like and are my cousins.

Marie leaned back. The ground was cool on her palms. She could not kick, so let herself fall instead. The earth felt cool on her back. Anyway, Marie said after a pause. I thought Ben was your only cousin.

Monette shrugged. That's just one copy of the word.

William and His Women Friends

drawing cards and counting paragraphs

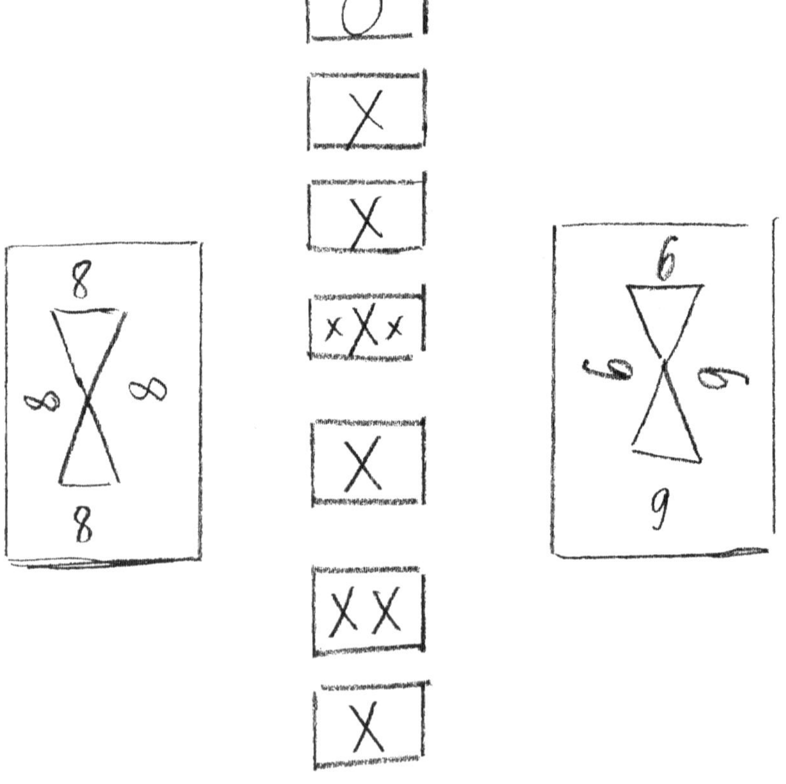

It is a horrible thing to be afraid, and William was afraid most of the time. Mostly, he was afraid of words, of using the wrong words at the wrong time, which generally meant saying the wrong things to the wrong people. There are many things to say and people who want to speak, though some are taught that speaking truth is ugly, rude, even hurtful. Were Kathy and Cathy fighting again? Did Delta feel ignored? William wanted to be a good friend. He wanted his friends to trust him and his broad understanding. He enjoyed the safe ache of a bruise pressed in the presence of another. In the sympathy space of one friend and one friend only, William could receive and reflect his friend's words, which made him feel safe and easy.

Alone, then, with his youngest friend, William listened to her confession. "My father ignored me," she sighed, "and became a certain kind of Republican. He believed the best girls grew up to be wives who serve their husbands, and while my husband pays the bills, it is I who set the tone. My unfeeling father created this great need for attention. He did not want me to become the person I am still becoming. William," she whispered. "I sense your dangerous intuition. You are older and wiser and know countless people with important connections. Will you be my friar? The salted earth I can stand on? Lend me your history and part of your name and I will speak louder for so many women." William loved the way his youngest friend spoke with such conviction. Even her rants felt like coos, drawing in sensitive young men and quirky straight women as deer to molasses. "Someone," she hummed, "must be the director of this, for as much as I want the world to change, centers still exist. I know what it's like to be the girl who needs permission." William believed in his young friend; when he listened to her, he wished he could sing.

William's friend Maryana knew the power of an excruciating bruise. She liked to make marionettes from newspaper, wire, and masking tape, staging small productions in her living room where she also kept a small, red-curtained stage. She glued her dyed-red hair to the head of one puppet and her sister's grey hair to the head of another. She dressed her William puppet in a crème-colored sweater and invited friends for a dinner party and play. "I have discovered a hidden method," she said. "When I pull these puppets' strings, I expose the social order. Here are the faceless puppets! They too want to be heard." She showed the guests one puppet draft after another. She said, "Here is my sister and here is me. Poverty and patriarchy make us do horrible things." The sister puppets looked out the window and screamed compliments at passersby, until the guests slowly left, one after the other. Later, Maryana spoke an elaborate story starring William and Maryana as big-hearted smarties who spoke out against daily manipulations. "But William," said Maryana, "I too want to be loved and accepted." "But William," mouthed Maryana's puppet, "when we came home from school, my sister and I often found our saint-like mother and babyish father sitting butt-bare naked, on the white leather couch." William's puppet turned its head and leaned his ear toward Maryana. "Oh William," Maryana wept. "We really are so brilliant!"

William's three older mother friends trusted him as a man of understanding. Their daughters called him Uncle William, and William, an only child, was happy in their claiming. The mothers were friends with each other, too, and while they hadn't planned on bearing daughters, they loved these daughters dearly. The older mothers told William about the challenges of raising children. "Now that we have daughters," lamented the mothers, "we can no longer sleep in or cry when we want to. We can't concentrate on making art or writing scholarly essays. The daughters' fathers don't help us like we need; they say we imagine our problems larger than they are. One father moved away and never sends money; another thinks that to be a mother ought to be enough; the final father feels sad about how society treats him. He writes a blog about feminist fathering and must spend time responding to his devoted followers. In the face of daily difficulties and absences, we focus on making better daughters." William loved the soft cadence of the mothers' complaints. He encouraged the mothers and helped the daughters, thoughtful girls who learned how to chop root vegetables when William and any one of the mothers made beef stew. When the daughters spoke, their soft words fell like sweet-smelling flowers at the feet of influential people, and William was happy to have arranged such meetings. The mothers told William he was a hero. "William," they sniffed, "our daughters might be redeemed."

To be a good friend to Delta was an especially delicate matter, for Delta was easily ruffled and often took offense. It wasn't that Delta did not care about the feelings of others;

rather, she experienced her own feelings so magnificently, she often forgot they were her feelings alone. When she visited William, she felt soothed by his petting and stroking. He made gluten-free meals while she told him her news. "Well, William," she mused, "I've heard that Alice is angry and Lucas feels he hasn't received his due. I'm not worried about Lucas; he's too savvy and emotive. But I don't want Alice upset, you know, she travels quite a bit and talks to very many people. Someone said that somebody told her I said something nasty. If I did, I truly don't remember." William nodded and served Delta some soy-free egg-drop soup. He loved the way she spoke so easily about so many subjects. With her, he became a frog held in the talons of a powerful eagle. "William," she wondered, "what's the difference between a friend and no friend? The one you love and the one you make love with? Can pleasure be measured, mounted, bound, and triangulated? The female sex has its own specificity. When a woman knows her body, she sets a revolution in flow."

Kathy and Cathy were fighting again, and William hated his spot in the middle. Yet when Kathy called, William went to her house without question. He found her in an upstairs room, sitting beneath a crimson-colored veil while gazing at the street below or maybe at nothing. William sat with her, silent, until the sun began to set, the sky filling pink and orange-red, and still, Kathy did not speak. William began to worry. It was not like Kathy to sit so long, so still, so speechless. Normally, she told wild stories about her adventures in real life and in literature, disregarding realism in favor of social and historical facts. Like fairy tales about young women who were raped by their fathers and brothers and blamed their mothers. Or fables about courageous abortion-seekers who cry wolf when they need to and will fuck with the lambs. William loved Kathy and her many stories, how she spoke so methodically, how she loved the other Cathy, who was even more severe in her critiques and very unrelaxed. William waited for Kathy to confide about Cathy, but when the sun fully set, the darkness all about them, Kathy stood and told William to go home.

There were so many things to say, but William hadn't said them. Normally, William greeted each day as a new beginning, and when he was with one friend, he didn't consider—he barely remembered!—the others. But when he had problems, like this worry over Kathy, he often telephoned his editor friend who sometimes told him what to do. That day, however, his editor friend answered and cried: "William! There is a giant spider who is trying to get me. I have spoken to many therapists about my irrational fear of spiders—I know they eat bad flies and someone once whispered that a spider wove the first alphabet within her web. So, intellectually, I know she opens the space into language and is my friend! But these heebie-jeebies make me nauseous. She's mammoth, a hairy spider whose yellow web crisscrosses my main doorway. William, I can't get out and don't know what to do!" William felt confused. Normally, his editor friend listened to William while mirroring his shifting tones and affects. It was a skill they shared, and when his editor friend howled and dropped the phone, William, still wordless, pushed the red button to end the call.

Using the wrong words at the wrong time was exactly what had happened. William was angry at his editor friend and angry, he realized, at Kathy. She wanted everything from him—his care, his thoughts, his attention—and for this, he got to be near her, that's all. But anger also felt upsetting, so he put on soft music and sat in a large reclining chair and there, he became sleepy. In his dream, a woman looked into his palms and saw a prisoner, sitting remorsefully, clad in brown. The prisoner's palms were hot, a single lightbulb hung above his head. The palm reader was small, with long dark hair and big black eyes. She said, "William, you have been too long waiting. I see a red squirrel, nature's furry hoarder, dead in the park—a sad corpse rotting above ground while no one gathers its piles of piñons, exactly measured according to need and hidden in the hollows of nearby trees. William!" she cried, and he woke and knew his dream was from another realm.

"It is a horrible thing to be afraid," wrote William in the morning. "Collecting and naming your fears does not change the alone."

&

Marie might if Monette will.
But will Monette go?
Will there be candy?
Marie shrugs.
Will we sing?
Marie smiles.
What about pop? Secret prizes? Can we hide beneath the benches?
They call them pews.
Are they smelly?
Like the pee inside you!
When Monette laughs, Marie will too.

&

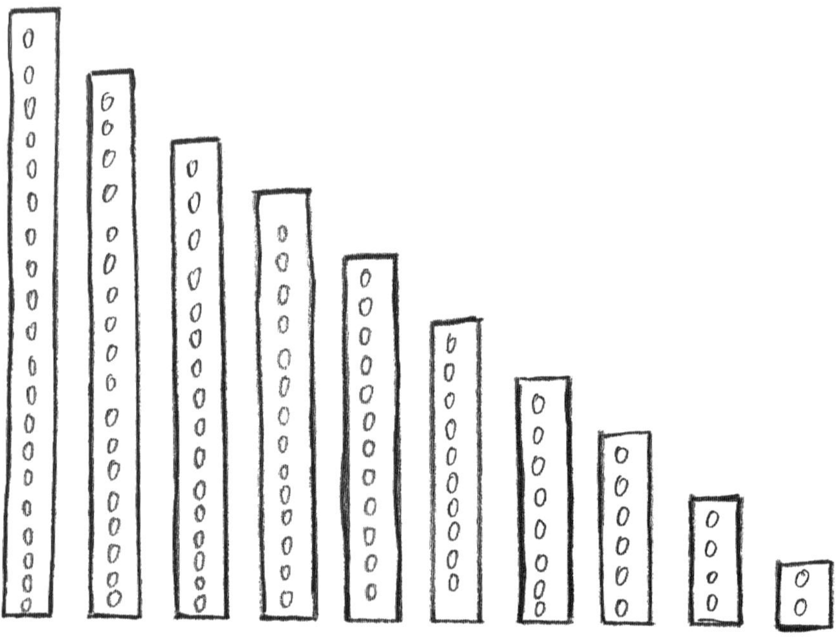

Marie Studies the Fine Art of Release

delete patterned repetitions to lessen what is carried forward

1.

Pastor Rauber warned against holding others' grievances as your own. You weren't the one wounded, he had said, so you have nothing to forgive. Marie felt something true about this particular teaching, even as others struck her as certainly false. He'd told Shannon, for example, that her son's leukemia diagnosis pointed toward a hidden sin she needed to confess. No, argued Marie: if God doesn't want you to carry other people's griefs, then God wouldn't afflict others for your transgressions.

+

It was Marie's second visit to the hospital that day. The first was for G, a young woman assaulted while walking home from The Pub. They lived in a small town and G was on the north end of Main Street—down the hill, past the stoplight, near the duplex apartment where Marie, twenty-five years old, lived alone without even a cat. G did not know the man who followed her as she left The Pub. Marie learned these details later because at the hospital that morning G did not want to speak, and it was Marie's job to make sure that if she did not want to, she did not have to. G had wanted the exam and for Marie to be there. She wanted Marie to talk to the cousin who had driven G to the hospital and was sitting in the waiting area. The cousin had curly hair and wore a red sweater with a polar bear on its front, that's how Marie identified her in the waiting area, amidst the slouching bodies in patterned blue chairs. Speaking to the cousin had been difficult; the cousin wanted to see G.

I'm sorry, Marie said, but G wants you to wait here. The cousin began to cry, her hair bounced with each sob. She had stayed at the bar to have another while G walked home alone.

I could have stopped it, said the cousin.

You don't know that, said Marie. She gave the cousin the crisis line number. Please call, she said. Someone can help you. We talk to friends and family, too.

I could have stopped it, repeated the cousin.

Stop, said Marie. You're here now. That's what matters.

During the exam, G held Marie's arm so tightly it bruised.

+

What if your story is bound with the stories of others? Is any story lived alone? Nearly fifteen years after leaving her job at the women's organization, Marie asked these questions of Lila, an older and wonderfully accomplished writer whose books of trauma and witness neither resolved nor redeemed. To Lila, stories were more like water than solid objects: they flowed from one person into another. Stories, Lila told Marie, are larger than *yours* and *mine*; they exist in the flux between wet and dry, over and under—a story happens, is happening, when a response becomes a call.

Which was not how Lila spoke of emotion, or energy in motion, for when it came to that invisibility, it was important, Lila explained, to know the feeling's source. And Lila knew. For she was also a healer: she read tarot cards and was a Reiki master. She knew when energy was blocked and could perceive the unexplainable. Like how in the story Marie was writing, the bear hadn't provided protection. How did Lila know about the bear in Marie's story? How, asked Lila, might the bear-image move? Marie was at Lila's house to consult about her novel-in-progress. Marie was beginning to understand writing and spirituality as necessary to each other's existence as figs to fig-wasps and the wasps to fig trees. Let your life and writing pollinate each other, Lila often said, for the extraordinary is always present, which does not mean it will reveal itself. It does not have to, Lila laughed. Write what scares you but remember: *sacred* and *secret* do not mean the same thing. Lila ended Marie's reading with a gifted flower essence tincture for balance, clarity, and courage. Now, said Lila, shall we eat? Marie nodded.

After lunch, Marie and Lila hiked in a nearby canyon. It was hot; the trail was dusty. Past a jutting rock, they turned a corner and Marie walked into a visceral memory of that day at the hospital, of G's cousin—the smell of beer and cigarettes on her unwashed body, tears and snot streaking her featureless white face. Marie felt a sudden bilious anger, heart clenched, breath captured. She wanted to weep but instead imagined slapping the cousin, the wet blankness of her cheek and a sting lingering in Marie's palm.

Marie tried to remember G's face, only to realize that G had become The Young Woman Who Left the Bar Too Early. The Young Woman Assaulted on Marie's Same Street. For Marie knew nothing more specific of G's story: if she went to court, began drinking more or less, stayed in the area or quit speaking to her cousin—how that night continued to live within her body, including if she, like Marie, eventually worked at an organization that helped people, mostly women, survive violence so familiar and expected we call it *domestic*.

In the canyon, Lila walked ahead of Marie. I'm amazed, said Lila with a small heelturn, the moment always gives us what we need. Just then, a bee landed on Marie's sunglasses, startling her into a stumble. But a happy one, for Marie attributed the felt imprint—the faceless image of G and her cousin, her stinging palms and the unstinging bee—to Lila's magic, as if Lila somehow conjured Marie's memories because Marie needed to... Marie felt something almost forgotten. She wanted to ask Lila about memory and if there was a dead someone—Nina? her grandma? Aunt Jean?—always around her, but by that point in their friendship, Marie had learned to wait for Lila's offers. Lila knew a lot of people and needed to be careful with her connections. To be taken in by Lila was part of her alluring charm.

+

Marie's more vivid memories were of the second rape exam that day. It was late afternoon and C, an older woman, shivered in the air conditioning. Marie grabbed her own hooded sweatshirt from the chair.

Here, she said. C didn't answer. Can I? asked Marie. C nodded and Marie draped the grey cloth over C's shoulders. Marie had bought the sweatshirt in high school, when she still wore makeup and refused to imagine the future because she didn't want a life of birthing babies, folding laundry, and feeding a husband, even if that's what people in her Midwestern hometown assumed a grown-girl's life would be.

C crossed her arms as she pulled the sweatshirt tighter around her. She looked older than Marie's mother. Her pale skin was thin; her jowls heavy; her hair frizzy and grey. There were dark spots on C's hands and forearms. Marie felt C's tremor as an omen in her bones.

It's like Dotty, C said. She looked at Marie with bleary blue eyes.

Marie pressed her toes into the soles of her shoes, trying to stay present. Who is Dotty, she asked.

I don't know Dotty, C replied. She stared at the floor or nothing in particular.

Can I rub your back? C nodded and Marie began a circular motion.

What about Dotty? C repeated.

I don't know Dotty, said Marie. There was a heavy pause. But it's terrible, Marie continued, whatever happened.

What happened?

I don't know.

I miss my mommy. C's voice began to garble.

Pressing her palm into C's back, Marie silently counted to four as she inhaled, held for two, counted backward from six with her exhale.

+

It was while Marie worked at the women's organization that she secretly began writing. Nothing serious, just playing around with words. She also started therapy and was avoiding her mother's infrequent phone calls. When she did call, her mother left the same repeated message: Well, it's me again. Just me. Nothing happened, nothing new. Marie lived on the West Coast, her mother still in Michigan, so the time difference gave Marie an excuse for not returning her mother's calls. When they did talk, every conversation circled back to her mother's dreadful fret: what she hadn't done that day, not enough or in general. Always never will.

2.

The nurse pulled the door closed. The doctor is coming, she said. When neither C nor Marie responded, she sniffed and scratched her shoulder, fixed her gaze on C. I know this is difficult, her voice even more matter-of-fact. She glanced at Marie. Let's be quick so you can go home.

Marie bit the inside of her lip; the nurse did not know. Marie moved closer to C and whispered. Not there, she said, not home. Marie pressed C's shoulder, gently.

C nodded. Started to drift as the nurse washed her hands at a corner sink and Marie studied the aquamarine of the nurse's scrubs. Wide shoulders, pear-shaped hips. The room was cold and bright.

C startled up. Where's the doctor, she asked.

She's coming, Sweetie. The nurse spoke over her shoulder.

Marie frowned. Sweetie? Why would the nurse use that term? Marie made a mental note to report this to the sexual assault services coordinator at the organization.

The doctor is female, then? Marie wanted to confirm.

Just said that, the nurse replied. The nurse placed a sheet of pale blue paper on the medical tray, avoiding Marie's gaze as she calibrated her watch against the clock on the wall and gathered supplies.

Just checking, said Marie. Too much edge in her voice. Breathe and let it go. Be there for C, who was slipping, Marie sensed, into a shiver. A blankness filled her eyes.

+

Three years later, Marie saw a similar look on her mother's face after she heard Marie's poetry for the first and only time, though given the venue—a women's art festival with many lesbians and odes to the pussy—Marie did not know if her mother was responding to the poems or to the festival itself, which took place in a small city near her mother's hometown. Marie was newly out—though not yet to her mother—and ready for her own odes and queer hookups, like that weekend with a singer-songwriter who lived nearby. It felt nice to be accepted into the festival, and while Marie did not consider herself a poet, she wanted to write grief in poetic forms tied tight enough to bruise, and she wanted to read poetry near her mother's birthplace, which felt a necessary turning of a corner. She hadn't, however, invited her mother to the performance because she knew that her mother, who still hated the word *ms* instead of *miss* or *mrs*, would not enjoy a feminist art festival. But Marie's aunt, her mother's older sister, saw Marie's name listed in a local newspaper article about the festival, and telephoned Marie's mom to exclaim that while she would be out of town and miss Marie's performance, she wanted to hear all about it when she returned. So, Marie's mother felt compelled to go, praying for protection and hoping her daughter might surprise her. Instead, Marie composed her set as if her mom wouldn't be there, with a poem about staining a library chair with menstrual blood and another about the first date rape, did that one count? As Marie finished her reading, she saw her mother hurrying toward the exit, her face triggered into blankness. Later, Marie's mother said the whole thing made her nauseous and Marie felt a vomitous unease gather in the back of her own throat.

+

By the time she met Lila, Marie had given up poetry for prose, and published a slim volume of fiction that collaged personal experience with biblical language, theory, and an imagined portrait of the reader: How are you like Dotty? wrote Marie. For that story, Marie based her protagonist on a cousin, who distanced herself after receiving the copy Marie had sent, along with a note about how impressionism is more about color and emotion than accuracy and mimesis. But Lila understood. She was the first stranger to send Marie an email about her book. It takes courage to see clearly, wrote Lila, and she invited Marie to participate in a speculative memoir event hosted by a literary organization in another state. Marie was flattered and willing, yes, to pay her own way. She deeply admired Lila's writing. She followed Lila on social media and listened to her podcasts, knew about Lila's growing and devoted fan base, how Lila was doing something about… this is where Marie hesitated. Does publishing these stories encourage and uplift others, she asked during the panel. Or are we here to sell books and become respected voices in the field?

A false binary, Lila declared. A symptom of the oppressor's logic, his white patriarchal worldview. Marie agreed, though confessed a feeling of never doing enough.

Lila responded as if the audience were absent. Isn't this, she said, why you write? To glimpse your horror's twin? Because, dear Marie, you are more than you realize. And there is nothing to forgive.

Then Lila told a story about her mother and grandmother, of a shock she could not fully speak, generations caught in the ongoing recollection. My mother, Lila said, was formed from a bilious anger. My mother, Lila said, warned me in her skull.

During the Q&A, everyone's questions were for Lila, which neither surprised Marie nor the other panelists for Lila had created a mesmerizing rend. After the event, Lila invited Marie to the hotel bar, where they drank scotch and soda in a corner booth. A double, please, and one more.

+

The doctor arrived; the exam began: 5:17 p.m., the nurse noted. The nurse wouldn't leave the room until it ended, as her continuous presence ensured the kit's legal validity. Marie explained this while reminding C that, no matter what and for any reason, she could stop the exam any time.

C almost nodded, eyes glazed.

The doctor was young with short natural hair and a calming voice. I'm sorry you're going through this, she said with warmth. The doctor paused. We'll go at your pace; it will help me to hear what happened.

C nodded, this time for certain. Marie offered her hand and C held it. Marie felt a flush of weariness. She wanted to be there; she wanted it to be over. The fluorescent lights buzzed brightness; the putty-colored walls pitted with spots.

Marie didn't notice the nurse shifting her weight from one foot to the other, blood pressure cuff in hand.

Can I? said the nurse. She looked at Marie.

She needs to take your blood pressure, said Marie. When C didn't respond, Marie released her hand and moved to the other side of the bed. She touched C's left arm. Is this okay? asked Marie. She glanced at the doctor, who was slowly drying her hands.

Can I borrow this arm? The nurse's voice was lower, softer. C nodded.

Marie watched the nurse squeeze the egg-shaped bulb that pressurized the cuff. As the nurse released the device, Marie realized she was holding her own breath. She exhaled a sigh and felt a slap in her skull.

3.

On the canyon trail, Marie stepped carefully while Lila spoke about a former student. Evidently, he had used Lila's name to book a reading for himself at a much sought-after venue in New York. When she confronted him about it, he accused Lila of writing about him in a series for the *Paris Review*.

That's weird, said Marie. She didn't want to inquire too directly.

He wasn't ready to read in New York, said Lila. The sky was a cloudless white-blue that stretched for miles.

What happened, asked Marie.

Lila left Marie's question alone. The path was covered in loose gravel, which Lila navigated with seeming ease in her vegan hiking boots, while Marie, in her tennis shoes, tried not to slip. The two women walked in silence.

Have you hiked here before, asked Marie. She paused to pick up a stick lying on the side of the trail, perfect for walking.

Lila stopped to gaze at the sandstone and jutting rocks, the open horizon. She stretched her arms wide and inhaled deeply; Marie relaxed for a moment and tried to quit worrying about whether they liked her and what that might mean. They, in this case, meant Lila, her husband, John, a reputable novelist who hadn't published a new book in over fifteen years, and Lila's college-age adopted child, Steven, who still lived with them. Or rather, in the mother-in-law apartment Lila had built over the garage, while Lila and John each had half of the duplex bungalow they'd bought when John accepted the job at the university. That was twenty years ago. They'd managed to get Lila a position there, as well, while maintaining an open relationship, though they kept that information private. Lila supposed that even Steven did not know. The stick felt smooth in Marie's hand. She couldn't help it; she liked being liked.

You look, said Lila, like the two of wands. The world in your hands.

Could Lila feel Marie's thinking? Writing, Marie will learn, has many teachers, not all of them for life.

+

The doctor rolled her stool closer to C, who sat at the end of the examination table, her feet rocking slightly, forward and back. Marie stood on C's right side, the nurse on her left.

Is this okay, asked the doctor.

I don't know what you mean, said C. There was a strange smell beginning in the room, not quite onion, not quite rancid.

The nurse sniffed and Marie wondered if she smelled it, too. She tried to lean into the scent, but lost it instead.

You can speak freely, the doctor said. Nothing is off limits.

Though it will, reminded Marie, become part of the official record. Evidence that may be submitted in court.

That's right, the doctor agreed. The room became deeply still while the air conditioning seemed to hum louder. In the hallway, something rolled by. So, continued the doctor, soft and careful. Tell me what happened.

C shook her head and swallowed. Marie knew bits from when she'd met C in the waiting area for the intake. She offered her hand; C held tight.

He said they were his cousins, C said. Her face crumbled and language fell apart, broke down. Sounds won't match marks on and in the body. Hard to hear but needed to listen. Harder to speak but needed it heard. Inside and outside. Repeated.

Date: yesterday.

Time: can't remember.

Location: I never did enough.

+

Like many advocates, Marie began at the organization as a volunteer. It wasn't just their work that mattered, but the organization's philosophy, how it came to be: from consciousness-raising groups in the early 70s, where women spoke about their lives and saw similar patterns—beliefs and be-haviors—come into view. Phyl, who worked at the business office, liked to share this herstory with the younger work-ers or volunteers. Phyl had been there at the beginning but didn't consider herself a founder.

It was the movement, Phyl said, that found us. Made the personal, political. Remember, Phyl sometimes said as she handed out paychecks: women weren't allowed to own checking accounts until the 1960s. Before 1974[1], we need-ed a husband's signature to get a loan. A pregnant person could be forced into maternity leave and lose her job, while landlords could turn down tenant applications for doubt that "she" could pay. We were considered too dotty to han-dle money, or even own our own bodies, because if we were married, our *no* didn't count.[2] Other times, Phyl told stories about the organization's early days, how all decisions were made by consensus. Everyone was a *coordinator*, and no one had more authority than another. That's how we conducted performance evaluations too—all the coordinators gathered in a room to give one coordinator her feedback. It was bru-tal. Phyl laughed. But VAWA[3], changed things. We had to professionalize to get grants, list a primary mission on our

---

[1] Phyl is referring here to the Equal Credit Opportunity Act, passed in 1974.

[2] In 1976, Nebraska was the first state to strike down the "marital exception" in rape laws; it took 13 years for marital rape to become illegal in all 50 states, with Oklahoma and North Carolina withdrawing their marital exception laws in 1993. In some States, the laws changed only because courts found the excep-tion to be unconstitutional.

[3] Violence Against Women Act, first passed in 1994. VAWA is up for renewal every five years. It was reauthorized in 2000, 2005, and 2013. It lapsed in 2018, presumably due to the US Federal government shutdown of 2018-19. It was reauthorized in 2022.

applications: help survivors or end systemic violence. It's a good use of money, Phyl said, but she sometimes wondered if Congress hadn't designed the funding rules to buy silence and compliance. And we're still, Phyl sighed, trying to get more women of color involved. They're just… Phyl's voice often trailed off.

Marie listened to Phyl while considering her own childhood—the seemingly de facto segregation of her neighborhood and schools, and how most topics weren't allowed in the church, much less at the table. Her mom treated sex like something wives owed to husbands, along with clean socks and home-cooked meals. In exchange, he paid the bills and didn't complain. That was part of the bargain—to stuff his feelings. Marie had watched her mother, always guarded, repeatedly pull away from her father before heading to Women's Bible Study, where they spoke about themselves as broken, needing to place more trust in a God who loved them so absolutely he required their total submission. Or he would, no choice, doom them to eternal hell.

At the organization, Marie learned about gaslighting and the 1940 film *Gaslight*; she studied pictures of the Drama Triangle and the shifting positions of victim, rescuer, and perpetrator. She saw where she stood in relation to others after a Privilege Walk and felt layers of perception coming into focus. She understood grief and bilious anger directed not just outward, but in. She saw words clustering into shape-shifting creatures: not aggressive, but assertive; not a bitch, but self-respecting; not about sex, but power. And no woman was ever *asking for it*, no matter how nice or unfriendly she was or the length of her skirt.

+

The lights buzzed. There was a bruise on C's neck. Marie stared until its red and purple turned into something else. A turkey's silhouette. Such a stupid bird. Marie wanted a different image, but it helped to focus. On something. The bruise became a bruise. Because he meant to. Slap cut punch. Like that game. He said, this is my cousin. He said, quit flirting with him. He said, show us a good time. C stopped talking.

Marie held C's hand, felt the chills running through her. Felt wrong and wronged. Nothing for me to forgive, thought Marie.

4.

After their time together at the speculative memoir event, Lila and Marie began emailing each other in earnest. Lila was so charming, her emails intensely intellectual and so beautifully written. She was interested in Marie's writing, but also in her work as an editor, how she felt about her literary friendships, including with her wife, Louise, who was increasingly out of town. Marie was lonely, she realized, and while she did not believe in her mother's god, she sensed there was more to living than the visibly material realm. Lila shared stories of her own awakening—to writing, yes, but also to the incantatory power of language. How a performance could be a ritual. How our connection to ourselves, our inner knowing, gets covered over with trauma, with culture, with bad words. When Lila had heard that Marie, with Louise, would be in the area because Louise had a weekend long performance at a small art gallery, Lila invited Marie, not Louise, to the house for a tarot reading, lunch, and the hike. Louise would be installing and rehearsing all day anyway, so it had worked out.

Marie parked the rental car in front of Lila's duplex bungalow, so cute with its seagreen shutters. As Marie moved toward the front door, Lila poked her head around the building's northwest corner.

Yoo-hoo, Lila called. Did you notice a prize in the garden?

Tucked within creeping blue flowers, Marie saw a package wrapped in brown paper. Lila was a rush of smiles and ease, lifting the package and pretending to read, not familiar language, but a series of stones taped to the paper.

It's for you, Lila exclaimed. She took Marie's hand and led her inside. Marie felt Steven's quick assessment, even as he avoided Marie's gaze. Marie smiled, increasingly self-conscious, wandered deeper into the forest. She opened the package to find a notebook and three metallic-colored markers. During lunch, she mirrored Lila and Steven's portions and pacing, repeatedly exclaimed about the deliciousness, took seconds even though she was not hungry, heard Lila and Steven talking when she left the room. There is nothing to forgive, said Lila.

Marie wondered at her tone.

+

Some things are worse when spoken aloud. Marie remembered that earlier at the hospital, the young woman, G, had also avoided the questions, even as Marie explained they were standard, necessary even, for the reports attached to the exam. G didn't want to talk to the police; she was angry when Marie explained she hadn't been the one to report the incident. The hospital did, as required by law. What can I say, G had said, I am always on guard. G had showered, too, before coming to the hospital. She couldn't stand to not shower, she said. Then silence. Though Marie sensed her bilious anger every time the nurse narrated the next part of the exam.

The afternoon nurse was different, noted Marie, and C was less visibly angry, more disassociated. Marie realized herself thinking, turned a corner back into the present breath. The doctor verbalized her observations, while the nurse wrote, her pen tapping the clipboard. C's eyes were closed, her breath was shallow. Marie felt the slipping, so imagined roots stretching from the soles of her feet, anchoring within the earth's firm dirt. This pushed away the blankness for another moment. The pen tapped and the overhead light softly buzzed. A rectangular fluorescent. In the corner, Marie noticed a stain on the ceiling. The size of a dime, color of tobacco juice. The next day was Monday; she wouldn't be on call. Could have an evening drink and one more, if she wanted. She felt a wave of guilt. Thought: Some believe others must die so they can live, while others think they must die to give life.

+

The last time Marie visited her mother, she saw Pastor Rauber across the church parking lot. He was walking toward his truck, body puffed like a piece of processed corn, eyes hidden beneath a red baseball cap. Did he know that Shannon's son, the one with leukemia, was still in remission? Marie and

Shannon had recently reconnected on social media, followed by a phone call, and Shannon was dumbfounded to learn that Marie's mom still attended that same church. One of the deacons, Shannon had confided, was having an affair with not one but two single ladies, and Pastor Rauber covered for him, while making one of the women leave the church. As if she's the one, Shannon said, who needed to repent.

5.

Not victim, but survivor. Marie had learned the one-in-four number during a self-defense workshop, though when she listened to her friends, she found that often two or three or four of the four of them had stories of harassment and assault. Some hadn't said yes; some affirmatively said no. Or were too young to do anything besides get older. Years of wanting affection yet fearing attention. Sometimes Marie wondered how she'd managed to live without feminism. Other times she wondered if she chose her friends because there was something—in their bodies, in their writing— that made them legible to each other. Their resilience and ability to turn a corner, to live beyond.

Marie's mother said she had forgiven the man who hurt her, but Marie didn't believe her. Was forgiveness even the point? As a teenager, Marie hadn't said yes to her boyfriend, even if some part of her wanted to. Voices like Pastor Rauber were too loud, around and inside her, they spoke of eternal damnation and original sin. Of the body as ill and corrupted. Of sad bad flesh.

Not sex, but power. Not desire, but domination. In the church and at the hospital. We're written in the flesh and from the flesh: we write.

+

Lila's mother haunted her writing, a good ghost who sang songs of political revolution to her baby girl, her only daughter. Lila's mother had died of breast cancer only a year after the death of her own mother, Lila's grandmother. Lila was sixteen years old, abandoned with a father caught in grief, eventually coffined by alcohol. He tried, Lila said, but her mother! Her grandmother! They were radical, feminist, leftist revolutionaries, and Lila spun their legacy as a desirable future.

Marie rarely spoke to Lila about her own mother and their complicated connection—the way they delighted and disappointed each other, often at the same time.

Who hurt your mother? This question was posed by another writer, during the event where Lila and Marie first bonded. Who hurt your mother? And Marie and Lila briefly, though definitively, locked eyes.

+

C began coughing, and Marie paused. The coughing worsened as the nurse shoved a kidney-shaped pink plastic container toward C, who sat up and spat yellow bile onto the bone-white floor. The puddle looked like a puddle, nothing more.

Are you okay, asked Marie.

C nodded.

Whoopsie daisy, said the nurse, voice too cheerful. She dropped a handful of brown paper towels over the yellow and squatted to wipe it up. When she tossed the towels into the trash, she changed her latex gloves, too. There, said the nurse. All clean.

C laid back down. I'm cold, she said.

Is there a blanket, asked Marie. The sweatshirt didn't cover much.

That feeling. A constant not enough.

+

Eventually, in her body, Marie will be able to name shame as the felt belief that you are wrong, regardless of what you did or did not do. Eventually, Marie will untangle shame from the wanting: allowing pleasure, a yes to joy.

6.

In the canyon, Marie and Lila found a rock large enough to hold them; they sat together, their feet not touching the ground. Lila pointed toward a mesa on the other side of the valley, noting its colors and layers of sediment. She reached out and covered Marie's hand with her own.

Marie heard her own breath, then a bird's trill, like the sound of falling or a spinning top slowly winding still. She hoped to glimpse the bird's body but opened her eyes to only canyon shrubs, their pointed mute-green leaves and small purple flowers. She glanced at Lila. Her hand felt hot.

Lila's eyes were closed. You're looking at me, said Lila. She did not move her hand.

Marie wanted to shift but couldn't. She flushed. She wanted to stay but wouldn't. She freed her hand to scratch her shoulder. Are you ready, she asked.

Oh, said Lila, eyes still closed. Your voice sounds weird.

Marie heard it, too. An uncommon pronunciation. More like song, less like home.

There are certain turns… Lila's voice was distant.

Marie felt her throat lumping, Lila's shifting body. The pulling away.

+

That's it, said the doctor, placing the final envelope into the kit. Fingernails, vagina, mouth, rectum. The nurse wrote C's full name on a sticky label, the pen had green ink.

C asked for a glass of water.

There's a cooler in the break room, said the nurse to Marie. Go left, turn the corner.

Would you like me to check on a bed? Marie focused on C's nod.

The hallway looked unfamiliar. Walls of blankness, where is the art? Christ raising Lazarus from the dead—hadn't she seen that picture walking in? She found Jesus in the breakroom instead. On the mound, talking about the humble. She filled a small paper cup with water and drank quickly. Almost done. She called the shelter, confirmed a spot. Relieved. She tossed her cup into the trashcan and grabbed another for C. She felt the paper cooling as it filled.

Back in the exam room, C stretched, arms forward. That hurts, she said. Her voice was gruffer in her everyday clothes. The nurse washed her hands in the chrome sink.

You can go home, now, said the nurse. Take a long hot shower.

C froze and Marie heard her own—No!—too loud, too sudden. The nurse glared.

Marie flushed. Focused on C. There's a bed at the shelter, said Marie.

Excuse me, the nurse said. Remember where you are.

Marie felt the familiar heavy, that no amount would ever be enough.

7.

How do we unburden ourselves? The question came from a woman with short hair and an impressive list of publications. But she was exhausted, she said, from the relentless minimization, the oversight and the othering. The hypervigilance, always watching, and the emotional labor of not losing one's shit in a culture that reads you with violence. When, she asked, would someone else have her back?

Lila wrote an essay about the woman's questions with this story as a response:

Two merchants lead mules down a winding path. The mules are overloaded with packages wrapped in brown burlap and tied to the mules' sides and backs. The merchants could be men or women or in-between, we do not know. Neither do we know their nationality or race, or if they inherited their wares, purchased them with hard-earned money at fair prices, stole them outright, or cheated others in a legal but morally questionable exchange. We have a sense of the merchants' present journey, but we cannot recall a specific point of departure. All we know is that the merchants are under excessive pressure; they are weary and overburdened. As are the mules. The mules must move slowly, matching each other's rhythm, which fuels the merchants' impatience. They want a prize hoped for just around the corner. The road is filled with blankness or potholes, meaning all four creatures—two mules, two merchants—must step carefully, must be constantly on guard.

But around the bend, ten bandits lie in wait. Wealthy bandits who steal from the poor or poor bandits who steal from the poor—we do not know. But the bandits want the merchants' goods. If the merchants continue along this path, the bandits will jump out, startling them and stealing all, thus relieving both merchants and mules of that which weighs them down, thus allowing immediate relief and the possibility of new ease. Even joy. But all four creatures will be hurt in the subterfuge. They were told to follow this path and will never know if the friend who gave this advice was intentionally deceptive, or simply unable to foresee such bad luck.

What should the merchants, what could the mules, do?

8.

Marie looked into her rearview mirror. C was still there in her fern-green car, so everything was okay. They were going to the organization's business office, where they would meet two of Marie's co-workers, one coming from the shelter and another who, like Marie, was on call. The two advocates would handle C's intake.

Marie noticed her tense shoulders and relaxed. It was 6:30 p.m. She would remain on call for another eleven and a half hours. She flashed on leaving the hospital earlier that day, the first time. The young woman and her cousin walked ahead of Marie. She lost sight of them as they turned a corner. Yet Marie could still hear the cousin's loud voice. I'm so hungry, the cousin had said.

Marie tried not to listen. God dammit, she thought.

God dammit, she said into the blankness of her car. She slowed and turned on her blinker. C did the same. Down the short alley, into the parking lot in the back.

Wait here, Marie said to C. She punched numbers on the lock, stepped in and quickly grabbed the car cover from the bench by the door. You can never be too careful, she said.

Marie and C covered the car together.

It looks, said C, like a package wrapped in brown paper.

Marie nodded. Smiled. C'mon, she said.

Thank you, said C.

9.

Leaving the canyon, the sun made a western sky of pinks and orange, rose purple. Marie noticed her shallow breath, pinched heart, felt wrong for wanting something she couldn't name. She slipped into a familiar fog. Forehead filled with blankness.

The women turned a corner and a wild turkey stood on the path, feathers fanned in a gleam of patterned brown.

What a wonder, exclaimed Lila.

Marie watched Lila instead of the bird, the sun illuminating the space around Lila's body as she snapped a photo with her phone.

In the future, when Lila and Marie are ex-friends, Marie will see Lila's picture attached to one of her recorded talks titled "Transcended Self: You Act and React on Behalf of Others." Marie will listen, hoping she exists within Lila's story, as Lila does in hers. But Lila will talk only of the wild turkey—they have excellent hearing but no external ears—and of writing. Of heavenly creatures who dwell in the porous surround.

10.

That's not blankness between the words, linking sounds, prayers spoken. Marie wrote a story like a burning spell, unbinding repetitions, extending forgiveness. Mother, daughter, cousin, friend: all shall be released.

&

Are you lying? said Marie.

Why would I?

Monette began hopping on her left foot. I can show you, if you want.

We're not supposed to, said Marie.

Says who?

You know.

Monette stopped moving. We won't break them, she said. She held her breath. If I show you, do you promise not to touch?

In the basement were hundreds maybe thousands of them. Bears and little girls, clown heads, mugs and praying hands. Tall capital letters that stood on their own. M for Monette. M for Marie. M for Monette's Mom, who knew how to make things.

It's called ceramics, whispered Monette. But Marie was looking at dust and light and wondering about that feeling. Of pinkie swears, moss, and faeries. If Tinkerbell was less boobied and 100% real.

&

Trash Talk, or the Parable of the Frenemy

meditating on a piece of trash every day for seven days

Every morning for seven mornings, Marie studied a different piece of trash near the front door of her apartment building. The trash reminded her of a woman she knew, but not for the usual reasons. The woman came from a wealthy and culturally established family, while the trash came from passersby and the other tenants in Marie's building, neither of which were wealthy nor culturally established. Too, the woman was adamantly against trash, for such a label, as she liked to explain, categorically determined an object for either a landfill or a garbage barge, and the woman resisted both wastelands by throwing away as little as possible. "Reuse, recycle, re-gift!" she said with a big wink, knowing these words had been said by others and often. As someone who worried about climate change, Marie was grateful for any effort to reduce a carbon footprint, and like the woman, she also believed "words mattered." Yet she wondered at the woman's techniques, or more specifically, her linguistic recyclings. Did they provide clarity or obfuscation, or some combination thereof? Marie knew this to be a question as old as Plato's distrust of poets and Christ's fondness for straightforward parables—at least according to certain stories Marie had heard about those two men. Yet when the woman's face rose in Marie's mind's eye not once but twice, triggered both days by a seemingly random piece of trash, Marie began looking for a pattern linking the trash to the woman and gave herself five more days. To finish the week.

But what did Marie see those first two days? When she walked out of the apartment building on what would become day one, she saw a Styrofoam plate stuck in the leafy bush by the porch stairs. The plate was white with meat-colored stains and a brown mush smeared over part of its edge. Marie leaned closer and smelled cheap cat food. She looked at her building—an old house converted into small irregular apartments—and wondered what neighbor had left the plate, and if it was for the stray gray who liked to sun on the porch and was missing a bit of his right ear. It had been windy the night before, which might explain the plate's unfortunate location. That's when Marie thought of the secretly wealthy woman and her cat, Cesar Chavez. He was a big cat, black and white with green eyes, and the woman always shortened his name to Chavez, never Cesar, to avoid misapprehension. If she was speaking to someone unfamiliar, she added the phrase, "the cat who lives with me." Once, at a reading to celebrate a new translation of Japanese avant-garde poetry, Marie listened as their mutual acquaintance, Janae, asked the woman if she ever referred to Chavez as "her cat." "No," said the woman, "I care for Chavez but he is welcome to leave as his heart desires." The woman glanced behind Janae to see who was coming into the room, which was, after all, her room, as she was hosting the event. "That's very posthuman of you," said Janae, and the woman gave a knowing laugh and walked away. "My dog certainly likes her pets," said Marie when the woman was no longer within earshot. Marie thought Janae smiled. Earlier, the woman had introduced the evening's performance by saying, "I have this house so I can hold these kinds of events." The woman said this exact sentence every time she hosted an event, and Janae, who was sitting nearby, looked at Marie with a look that seemed to say, "Really?" The house did seemingly hold more rooms than events.

Marie had heard stories about how the woman fought her ex for full ownership of the well-located bungalow, which they'd bought and fixed up together. Yet by most accounts, the ex had done the bulk of the manual labor. And everyone said, too, that the woman had a trust fund, which explained why she could travel so much while working only part time. Not that the woman ever mentioned having money; instead, she liked to complain about how expensive things were, and when she traveled she always tried to find a local acquaintance she could visit, snagging an airport pick-up or free place to stay. In other words, the woman often benefited—personally, financially, or professionally—from her friendships. Looking at the woman's life, Marie could no longer tell these areas apart, so that her life seemed either a holistic flow of intentions and interests, or deeply com-promised, where every situation paid off with personal gain. Which is why, at least to Marie anyway, the woman's com-ment about keeping a house as a site for community smelled a bit like cat food left outside in bad weather.

But as Marie picked up the Styrofoam plate and placed it on the edge of the porch, it occurred to her that perhaps the woman needed to say such things—not to hide or im-press, but to keep herself honest, more or less. Perhaps the woman wanted to avoid becoming like her quite wealthy parents, who ordered others around and assumed they had the right to stand wherever they happened to be. Maybe these carefully chosen words helped the woman align herself into the relationships she'd like to have—with others and with the house itself, not as a possession or unwarranted prize, but as a person, a place, she cared for. So what is the sin here, thought Marie. Ah, the sin of abstinence, which for many isn't a sin at all.

Yet it was difficult to hold these more generous thoughts about the woman, especially on day two as Marie peered at an empty dried mango bag lying near the same spot as the cat food plate from the day before. The bag was from Trader Joe's and had what appeared to be teeth marks on both sides. She remembered the woman saying that she personally avoided "Trader GMOs" whenever possible, preferring the farmer's market near her house, which was more—and here the woman used the Spanish word for "practical" or "down to earth." Marie rolled her eyes just thinking about the woman's smooth confidence as she spoke. After all, everyone knew how great the farmer's market was, and that it was better to support small organic growers and to buy locally made artisanal jams and baked goods. But the farmer's market was too far for Marie to drive, and it was too easy to say the woman somehow believed that shopping at the farmer's market, and not Whole Foods or Trader Joe's, made her more conscientious and genuine than her peers. And it wasn't as if the woman wasn't interested in acquisition; her house/event site was filled with curios, which, while not indicative of wealth, bespoke the ability to globally flea market and thrift shop for things perfectly, delightfully, *ordinary.* The small everyday people, the woman often said, are the same ones who are systematically overlooked, oppressed, and forgotten. Yet Marie also watched the woman carefully add names of select individuals and cultural organizations to her circle of citations, and if a writer or artist began receiving a certain amount of attention, the woman could be counted on to already know the person and to consider her/him/them "a dear friend." "We should collaborate," the woman often said when meeting someone she wanted to be associated with. "I feel collected," commented one of Marie's friends after her first, and decidedly only, dinner with the woman.

This was the sin of avidity, which was, Marie realized, the other side of wrath.

Although what wrong did the woman do? Certainly, she was never a smoker, noted Marie on day three as she picked up an empty pack of Marlboro smooth menthol 100s from the ugly crushed stone covering the building's grounds. Marie suspected there was something not quite trustworthy about a person who had never smoked in earnest. Especially when the person was close to Marie's age, as the woman was, which meant they were teenagers and college students before the tobacco companies, in a major legal settlement, agreed to curtail altogether direct marketing to impressionable youth. When she was young, Marie hadn't known many nonsmokers, and the ones she had encountered exuded a certain amount of overly adjusted ambition. They were the children of parents with means and education enough to not only pay for their college education, but to praise their children's abilities and interests as well. The sin of generosity. The woman's parents had, in fact, always encouraged her to participate in art gestures and social causes, as befitted their own charitable inclinations, and the woman learned from them how to easily meet the most influential people in a room while adroitly avoiding eye contact with the less important. Too, the woman spoke three languages fluently, and liked to arrange and make things that were as visually pleasing as they were useful, from small editions of chapbooks assembled from repurposed junk mail (some of which Marie found on day four), to knit wrist warmers perfect for keeping cozy while bicycling to other houses for other curated events. And because the woman truly enjoyed working with others to create (only) positive change, she happily teamed up with any number of similarly socially minded artists to experiment with publications and performances ("reimaginings"). These always emphasized process over product and the everyday over the grand gesture, and always left Marie with a sad, small feeling inside.

But perhaps that was the point: to experience oneself as nothing more or less than the other people around you, including those who may be worrying over unpaid bills (just as Marie often was) and those who considered bills mostly a bother (paperwork), but showed up in this shared space for this shared time nonetheless. This, Marie decided, was the sin of activity.

On day five, Marie didn't notice the shards of broken pottery until she returned from her morning walk. The bright orange pieces had been a flower pot, abandoned on the porch by a former tenant, and while Marie had moved the pot from floor to railing months ago, she somehow never managed to fill it with dirt and a tulip bulb. The evening before, she settled on Edith Wharton's Mrs. George (Bertha) Dorset as the woman's fictional equivalent—Bertha Dorset, who came from and existed within society, who knew what rules to break and was often a topic of gossip, admired even as she irritated and snubbed, and who would never be, for any reason (Marie was certain), excluded or fully pushed out of her circle. As for herself, Marie didn't identify with any of Wharton's characters (she doubted the woman did either), and while she found Lily Bart's downward spiral to be excruciating, she also thoroughly enjoyed Miss Bart's capacity for leisure and social intrigue. Yes, Marie thought, *The House of Mirth* is certainly bourgeois literature. She'd had this very discussion with the woman, who was, as a rule, critical of conventional narratives, excepting those written by members of marginalized communities and who were still, as the woman said, finding their voice. At the time, Marie had simply nodded and thought the woman condescending. But why, Marie thought, didn't she argue back? Marie knew she was as prone to turf wars and accidental power struggles as anyone, especially when taken by surprise. Just that morning, she had crossed the street to throw her dog's waste into a garbage can. An older Black woman sitting on her back porch yelled at her, saying "I don't want that in there." Marie, who was white and much younger, pointed out that it was in a bag, and the woman said that she didn't care and told Marie to fish it out. Marie did, but grimaced (she thought) at the woman before she left, to show the woman that she was unreasonable. And now Marie was mortified. Why had she made that face? Why had she thought dumping her dog's waste into the woman's trash was all right, especially as Marie saw the woman sitting on her back porch before she did it and could have easily asked her permission and been denied, which would have been far less shameful, especially in retrospect. But even in this, Marie thought, she herself might be committing the sin of remission. Her only consolation was glimpsing her own entitlement (she could and would do better, she determined), while perhaps giving the woman a good story to tell, one in which the woman was absolutely right while Marie was clearly wrong.

On day six Marie saw a cigarette butt and a wrapped piece of peppermint candy lying near each other on the pine needle-covered dirt. The pine tree wasn't directly in front of her building, but she liked to stand there with her dog and look into the tree branches. She was thinking about a Bible story she never learned as a child because it appears in a chapter of Daniel that Protestants consider apocryphal and so leave out. It is also the only Biblical story of a woman falsely accused, which means that, at least in the Bible of Marie's youth, any woman accused was guilty as hell. In the omitted story, the beautiful and God-fearing Susanna is married to the rich and well-respected Joakim. Every day, two elder judges visit Joakim to consult on a variety of matters, and over time the two men begin lusting after Susanna. They notice she often walks in the garden at noon, sometimes alone, and they begin leaving Joakim's counsel early, bidding goodbye to each other only to rush back, separately and secretly, to watch Susanna walk. One day, Susanna decides to bathe. She sends her maids away and locks the garden door. The two men, who have discovered each other's hiding place and their shared lust, decide to entrap her. "Lie with us," they say, "or we'll say we spied you with a younger man." Susanna refuses and, as she knows will happen, she is accused, tried, and condemned to death. There is more to the story, including how God chose a young person as the truth-speaking vessel before a bloody ending that redeemed the falsely accused while killing the lecherous lying grown-ass men. Contrarily, in *The House of Mirth*, Lily Bart takes an ever higher moral stand, but her good deed is never publicly known and no one finds salvation, including Miss Bart herself.

That night, Marie went to a party the woman was co-hosting in honor of Sam, the woman's "former student, now good friend," a hierarchical designation Maire suspected the woman would spout for years to come. The party was a backyard potluck and Marie brought a bag of Star Bright peppermint candies, which the woman uncomfortably called "truly and strangely unique" as Marie placed the open plastic bag on the table, next to someone's hummus. The house belonged to the other host, an artist Marie didn't know, though in the email invitation the woman described their recent text-image collaboration—a collaged critique of American imperialism (it's bad). Guests could wander into the artist's studio (a converted garage) and see this work alongside prints by the guest of honor. "We are so lucky to have Sam joining our community," said the woman, having instructed everyone to sit on blankets spread across the lawn. There were lights strung above them and around two trees, and Janae, who was sitting with Marie, whispered that she was glad to have her sweater. "Sam's work pushes viewers into new territories," said the woman, "and in the spirit of this work, we wanted to give Sam, and everyone here, a chance to meet differently." Marie glanced at Janae and zipped up her own hooded sweatshirt. The woman passed around a small bowl, explaining that everyone should choose a slip of paper. Each one contained a question written by one of the hosts—the woman, Sam, the artist—which they agreed would be a more interesting way to equally share everyone's interiority. "If you don't like your chosen question," said the woman, "you can also opt to tell a story of a memorable encounter with art." Marie looked at her question and knew she wouldn't address it. And the only stories she could remember at that moment were memorable for reasons she didn't like to say. Janae remarked that this was certainly different. "Yes," said Marie. "Sometimes there is the sin of goodwill." Janae gave Marie a strange look. "Is that a sin?" And Marie, who felt her own compulsive friendliness, said it depended on intention, now, didn't it? "The old theological debate," said Janae, "about what counts toward salvation: thought or deed."

When it was Marie's turn to talk, she said that her first experience of art was at the Bellagio in Las Vegas. "I was twenty-five years old," said Marie. "It was a Picasso exhibition." She paused. "It was neat."

The next morning, Marie found an opened condom wrapper, coconut-flavored, condom gone. It was a glimpse into a private action that told Marie nothing. She remembered how people laughed when she mentioned the Bellagio, thinking she was being ironic. She remembered the time she'd watched the woman as they sat in the same audience for an academic panel on race and gender identity in contemporary poetry. The woman was knitting as she listened, and Marie felt the tightness in the woman's chest and wondered what had happened to make her so anxious, so uncertain about whether or not she was good.

That was day seven, the sin of humility.

&

In the woods, near the fence, under the cedar and beneath the oak, above the grass and across the field, past the rock and inside the ravine between the hills, around the prickers behind the moss, at the spot called secret, Marie and Monette made soup. A bucket of rainwater, five leaves, three stones, a matchstick from the box with the red and black crisscross. The soup was not clear; the soup was not muddy. The girls added fingernails, a lock of hair, a drop of blood. One two, one two. Take a bite. Take a drink.

&

Carol Krusen Helps a Friend

using the language of the monomyth

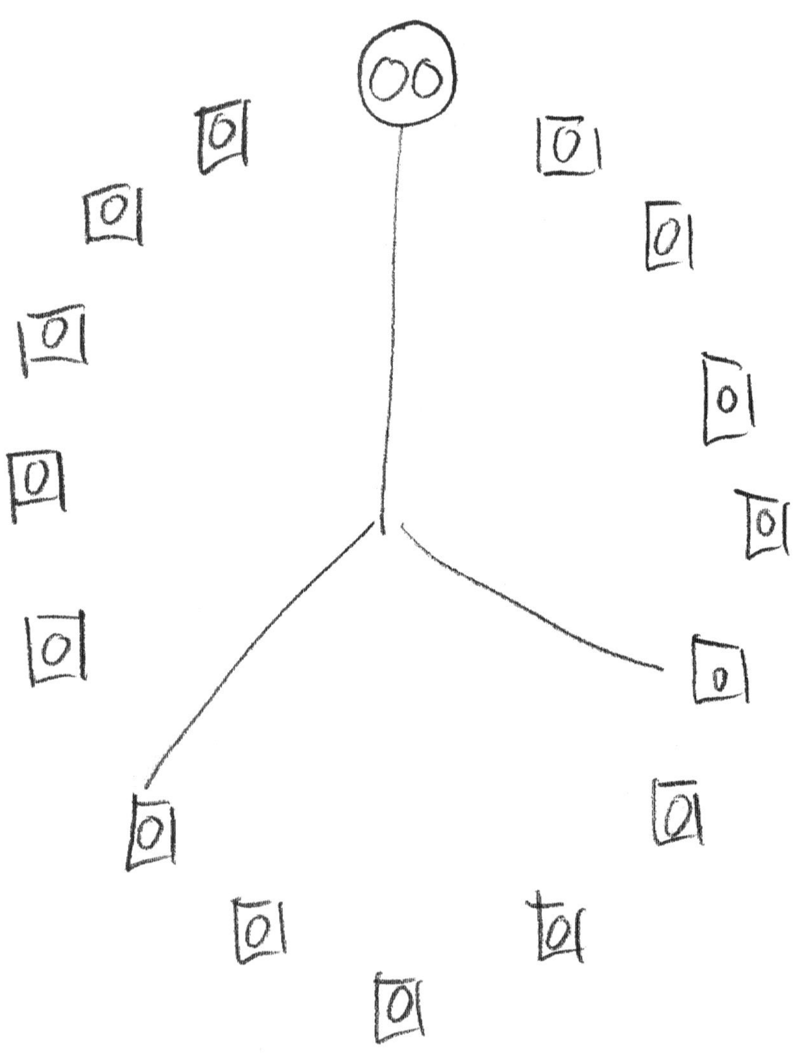

Part One: Departure

The first time Marie went home after college graduation, her friend Carol Krusen, who was her best friend in high school and her neighbor since birth, told Marie that she was pregnant and asked her to help plan the wedding. Of course, said Marie—because she loved being needed more than love itself. And nothing, she told Carol, could stop her from helping her absolute best friend through this big life change. The adventure begins, she cried, which is when Carol Krusen clarified that actually, she and Brad had already eloped that spring. But Carol had only agreed to drive down to Columbus, Ohio—where witnesses aren't required and there isn't a waiting period between applying for and receiving your marriage license—after Brad promised a proper wedding ceremony when Marie was back in town. Because Carol Krusen said she could not imagine getting married if Marie was not there, never mind the fact that technically she did just that.

Not that Marie necessarily cared about being present for the actual legal event. Plus, Marie secretly knew that if Carol Krusen hadn't already married, she would have tried to talk Carol out of this particular knot. Refuse him, Marie imagined herself saying, before launching into her reasons. Marie had made a list: (1) Twenty-three is too young to know what or who you want to be for the rest of your life, and (2) Brad's pretty aggressive, a bit of a bully even. (3) He likes to start arguments on socially explosive topics, especially politics and religion, as if offending others makes him more masculine, which (4) suggests an insecurity that will only lead to more of (2) and (3). And look, Marie would have continued, I get that he's intelligent but grew up so fucking poor that no one saw him that way, and now there's overcompensation. But he's become a thirty-two-year-old man who forces others to concede his point, which seems pathetic and certainly not wise or well-advised. Plus, he has an ex-wife, three children from that marriage, and a diagnosed mental illness that he self-medicates with alcohol. Carol Krusen, she would have said several times, this is not a good choice. But Carol knew these things about Brad. Details! she would have laughed. Besides, Carol Krusen was in love. Some things in life you simply will choose—because it's right even if it looks wrong, horrible even, when compared to a looks-good-on-paper kind of list, such as a steady income, mindful listening, a college degree.

Marie began to assist Carol Krusen with her wedding preparations, and the biggest challenge, aside from the rush (they only had six weeks before Marie would return to the West Coast) was finding Carol's dress. Not because Carol Krusen was a fussy woman—no one could accuse her of that—nor because of her tall full-bodied figure and enormous breasts, which would, by the time of little Emily's birth, reach a nursing size G, larger, as Carol Krusen would then point out, than little Emily's little head. Rather, the challenge was how Carol's whole body pulsed with her pregnancy, transformative and truly supernatural, so that a perfectly fitting dress on Tuesday would be lousy by Thursday, becoming too big, too small, too short, ridiculously long, or tight in the arms and strangely too loose in the chest. Something odd was happening, observed Marie, while Carol Krusen offered a knowing smile and mentioned her heightened sense of smell, as is frequently reported during pregnancy but rarely believed. That's it, cried Marie, we'll use your body as our guide. If we find a dress that fits perfectly enough on three separate visits, that is the dress for you. Carol Krusen agreed, and on the day of her wedding she wore this magically selected dress, found on week 31 of 40, for nearly eight hours. It was layered and full, beaded and gauzed, tucked, gathered, laced, and fastened with buttons that looked like real pearls. Brad was pleasant that day, close to agreeable, and Carol Krusen's father kissed his daughter on her cheek and said she looked like a puffy white present. Carol Krusen felt her own dead mother smiling down, just like in the pictures.

In the months and years after their wedding, Brad and Carol Krusen cycled through a series of beater cars and food stamp applications, even as they maintained their steady delight in each other, their willingness to disregard certain social norms. Brad quit drinking and Carol Krusen became a La Leche breastfeeding activist. Brad went back to school and Carol Krusen began researching homeschooling for little Emily: they didn't want their child to pledge allegiance to such a militaristic flag. Brad was "father" and "husband," while Carol was "mother" and "wife." They felt, Marie observed, quite pleased with themselves and each other.

Meanwhile, Marie had moved to the Pacific Northwest and worried about what to make of herself, being the first in her family to earn a college degree. She didn't want to follow Carol Krusen into the woods of motherwife, but neither did she have a specific career goal or occupation in mind. She felt herself lingering before a threshold into the great unknown that she feared crossing over. So, she made herself small and manageable instead, first, by moving in with a socially ambitious and reasonably attractive guy who refused to introduce her as his "girlfriend," and who insisted that she not change anything in the apartment, except if she was laundering the towels or sheets. Which isn't to say that he expected her to do his laundry; he would continue to do that himself, once a month, as was his current schedule. He would also continue his daily habit of wearing black eyeliner and eating dinner out, at the same cycle of restaurants every week: Mondays at the pizzeria, Tuesday at the taqueria, and so on. Marie was welcome to join him; he emphasized "her choice," and if she could not afford this luxury, he would pay. After all, he worked in tech. Marie was bothered by the way she sometimes felt ignored, but she also admired his refusal to play "partner," and she certainly wasn't going to cook for some man, and thus believed their relationship to be better than those who compulsively followed "traditional" gender roles. Basically, Marie found a certain comfort in this domestic situation, and given her own authoritarian father, she was used to working around a man's rules. She also convinced her boyfriend, whom she affectionately called Muggins, to let her build a five-foot-tall platform for his—now their—futon mattress, underneath which she would store her belongings undetected.

So, Marie built the platform and began eating dinner out every night, for which Muggins mostly paid. She applied for jobs and read several novels about people, mostly women, trying to find their way. She took guitar lessons, pottery lessons, voice lessons, and tap. She waited for something to happen, all the while feeling as if she were hanging out in the belly of a whale, not necessarily Biblical.

Part Two: Initiation

The second time Marie went home was after having an abortion, a procedure she'd scheduled the week before beginning her first post-college position at the local health department. Marie's eldest sister, Marsha, who knew little of Marie's actual life, asked about Marie's new "professional" job. They were eating dinner—beef patties with salad—and Carol Krusen was there, along with little Emily but no husband Brad. When Marie hesitated, Carol Krusen chimed in, practically singing, yes please tell them about WIC. The women at the table already knew that WIC stood for Women, Infants, and Children, because most of them—Marie's older sisters and Carol Krusen—relied on WIC food vouchers as part of their monthly household budget. Marie knew this and felt embarrassed. Not because she believed there was anything wrong with receiving WIC; two of her co-workers were also income qualified, and the program did a lot of good, even if it indirectly subsidized agribusiness by not allowing organic milk, which Marie also knew. But Marie, still uncertain about life's larger mission, was certainly determined to not need WIC herself, which she recognized as a bit of judgment, though she didn't want to position herself as an "expert" either, just because she sat on the other side of the WIC desk. Thus consumed with her own feelings,

Marie didn't recognize this moment as one turn on a road of more trials to come, and instead of answering honestly about what it was like to work there, which would have involved describing things and people not always with approval or understanding, she laughed off her sister's question, saying they (at the table) probably knew more about WIC than she. This made everyone vaguely uncomfortable, including Marie's sister, Linda, who muttered about what can and should not be discussed, before the family turned their attention elsewhere.

Marie tried not to care about sharing her news with her family. After all, she had Carol Krusen, and Carol Krusen was learning the Wise Woman's Way, a guide for alternative healing. She told Marie all about it a few days later as they sat in Carol's kitchen, little Emily playing on the cracked yellow linoleum floor. We aren't the only beings with intelligence and higher consciousness, said Carol Krusen in a confidential tone. If you listen, plants will teach. Marie nodded, encouraging Carol to go on. Carol Krusen began telling a story about walking in the wooded park with little Emily when they found a wild raspberry thicket. Marie flashed on an afternoon when she and Carol were still young and together, they ate as many raspberries as they could find from Carol's mother's garden. When Carol's mother saw their red mouths and sticky hands, she spanked both girls and sent Marie home. The berry-eating had been Marie's idea, because there were so many and because they were so good, but later she learned that Carol Krusen's family had less freezer jam that winter and Carol's father often blamed the girls, in a teasing tone, for his dry and tasteless toast. The raspberry leaf, said Carol Krusen, is a pregnancy goddess. She tones your uterus and birth canal while keeping your man at home. Marie smiled and said it was also probably less expensive than a gym membership. Marie was noticing the chipped paint and uneven cabinets—when Carol Krusen and Brad had rented this latest small house, they said that it was likely so inexpensive because it wasn't up to code. Marie, said Carol Krusen, please make yourself a motherwort tincture. It will help heal your anxious mind and soul.

Marie liked the idea but knew she wouldn't do it. Listen, she said, did you receive my letter? Carol Krusen kept every single letter anyone had ever sent her, starting from when she was four years old, sorted by date, bundled in yearly stacks held together with repurposed rubber bands, which she stacked in a bottom dresser drawer. Marie was fifteen the first time she saw Carol Krusen's letter collection and had practically fell over with envy at the organization and thought of it all. How had Carol Krusen known at such a young age that her letters were important and deserving? Marie's own system was to fill shoeboxes with cards she didn't want to throw away in case it hurt the other person's feelings. That letter, said Carol Krusen with a pause. I know you wrote that it was private, but Brad was there when I opened it; he grabbed it from my hand. Carol Krusen laughed as Marie blushed. Brad says you're too easily tempted, your perspective thoroughly skewed. But Carol, cried Marie, I wrote that letter only for you! I know, sighed Carol Krusen, and he knows he shouldn't have read it. But you must understand the way we share everything. Anything you say to me is something said to him. I won't have marriage with secrets.

For the next two days, Marie could think of nothing else. She was angry at Carol Krusen and felt humiliated, she realized, because she had been battling Brad for Carol Krusen's loyalty and affection, and Brad had clearly won. In the abstract, she agreed with her friend's desire for a "share-all" marriage, but Marie's secrets were not Carol's to share, just as Marie didn't share Carol's, even with people who were very unlikely to ever meet or know her. When Marie saw Brad a few days later, he warned that he was going to give her unsolicited advice: You need to settle down and marry, he said. Marie shook her head, no way, and when Brad asked, why, what's wrong with the man you're living with, Marie didn't reply. They were standing in the backyard, cooking chicken thighs on a portable grill, while little Emily sat in an old stroller pointing and saying bird. Carol Krusen called for Marie to help in the kitchen, and as Marie stood to go, she didn't mean to give Brad such a dirty look. Hey lady, don't take your man-issues out on me, he said. And Marie, who sensed that claiming her own authority would also bring atonement, for what, she wasn't sure, glanced at little Emily and smirked.

So later that day, when Marie told Carol Krusen about her abortion, she knew Brad would also soon know. And while she figured that Brad was the kind of man who believed women should have the right to choose even as he would never support his own wife or girlfriend making that choice—because life is beautiful, especially his baby's life—Marie was not prepared for Carol Krusen's response. Which was silence. A long silence. Followed by: having Little Emily helps me see things differently, more clearly, and I'm sad you won't have that and she won't have your daughter as her best friend. Marie scowled and replied that she wouldn't have moved back anyway, meaning their daughters, if that's what she would have had, wouldn't have been neighbors and maybe not even friends. Carol Krusen only smiled and said of course they would have, no question, and maybe Marie would have moved back. Who knows? The thought repulsed Marie, who had known since childhood that she could not live her big life in Michigan. How could Carol Krusen not know her like that? No, Marie said, I'm not moving back. What was the use, she later thought, of telling Carol Krusen how I am. Carol Krusen, who saw "mother" as the apotheosis of "female," and "me" as always "we." Resigned to forgo an ultimate boon, Marie prepared to return to boyfriend Muggins and to her life on the West Coast. She went grocery shopping with her mother and made spinach lasagna for one more family meal. She babysat her numerous nieces and nephews and took a last walk in the woods, where she stopped beneath a large oak tree and listened to the wind. What, she wondered, but couldn't think of an end to that sentence that wasn't sappy or sad. That last night at Carol Krusen's house, Marie had taken several photographs of little Emily, promising to send copies of the prints. Carol Krusen had placed an orris root in Marie's hand. To help you uproot that which is hidden, she said.

Part 3: Return

The third time Marie went home was seven years later, after coming out to her mother, who had told Marie she was deceived, not gay; at the time of Marie's visit, her mother still refused to see her daughter in any other way. So, Marie, who sometimes confused love with being needed, decided to focus her mother's attention on projects around the house and suggested they make a list, which both women loved to do.

Her mother's eyes brightened, and on the back of an envelope she wrote:

1) trim trees near barn

2) clean the garage

I want to get rid of stuff, just get rid of it, said Marie's mother. Okay, said Marie. Do you want to have a garage sale? Her mother said maybe, maybe she should have a garage sale. Should she have a garage sale? Marie said she didn't have an opinion either way. If her mother wanted to have a garage sale, she would help. If not, they wouldn't. Oh, I should probably have a garage sale, said her mother, as she penned a square around her two-item list. Mom, you don't need to have a garage sale, replied Marie. I don't have to have a garage sale? said her mother. Marie sighed. I don't want to, said her mother. I don't want to have a garage sale. Then don't, said Marie, suddenly hating the "garage" part of the sale. Why not call it a sale? suggested Marie. But her mother continued talking: I'll have your brother come over with his truck, that's what I'll do, and haul this stuff to the dump. Marie glanced at the pile of unopened mail fanning the table, solicitations, mostly from Christian organizations who were saving the world from people like Marie. The dump? said Marie. That's not good enough for you, said her mother. Mom! cried Marie. She wanted her mother to stop. Is this why you refused to return for so long? said her mother. While they were talking, Marie's mother had filled the rest of the gas bill envelope with doodles of flowerpots and blooming plants, and a couple of what looked like lightning bolts.

Marie's second eldest sister walked in the front door. Hello, said Linda. Do you want to go garage-sale-ing? Everyone laughed. We were just talking about garage sales,

Marie said. Mom doesn't want to have one. Oh, they're a pain, said her sister, who sat at the kitchen table and pulled out a deck of playing cards. She dealt herself a game of solitaire and began talking about her new neighbors. Horrible people, she said, just horrible. They tore down the fence between our yards because they said it was ugly. But that was *my* iron fence, continued Linda, and now *their* dog runs into *my* yard. This morning, I told them if *they* don't fix it, I'll let *my* kids use *their* dog as a BB gun target. Not Magic! the neighbors cried. What kind of people call their dog Magic? Come, Magic—Stay, Magic—It's the stupidest thing I've ever heard. But even worse, explained Linda, was how her husband, Steve, helped them with a plumbing emergency and now they refused to pay.

What's wrong with people, said Marie's mother. It was later in the day and they were cleaning the garage. Her mother's garden tools hung in an organized pattern spray-painted on one of the walls, which reminded Marie of Carol Krusen's mother, who always kept everything so neat, so tidy, and Marie and her mother began to talk about the Krusens. Mr. Krusen had passed away the year before, Marie's mother reminded her. Marie hadn't spoken to Carol Krusen for over three years. Will you see her this time? asked her mother. Marie shrugged. And what about Muggins? though Marie's mother used his real name, which Marie had never liked, because it felt untrue. He had, Marie told her mother, married someone who loved to make pies and they were living in Portland. They didn't talk about Marie's wife or her wedding nearly five years before. Like Carol Krusen, Marie had crossed a border (in this case, national) to marry in a place (Canada) that had different legal rules. Marie's family did not approve of any of it and when Marie told her mother about the marriage her mother only said that she had been worried Marie might do something like that. Carol Krusen, on the other hand, had been pleased that Marie had finally settled down. It's better to be married, isn't it? said Carol Krusen. For everyone? said Marie, and Carol Krusen laughed deep and long. Marie realized that Carol Krusen viewed marriage as rescue from without, a way to return to the everyday childhood life of family, but with new knowledge, new choices. New skills. And Carol Krusen wasn't totally wrong about that, Marie now realized.

I think I will call Carol Krusen, said Marie to her mother, and later, on the phone, Carol Krusen told Marie that she was welcome to come visit, but Carol, herself, couldn't leave home. Carol Krusen's voice sounded as sure and as warm as it always had, and she was happy to tell Marie her news. Little Emily was strong and healthy, and Brad was working on a second degree. They were growing vegetables, raising chickens, making their own homespun clothes. And I'm pregnant, she said. Or rather, I'm carrying Baby Z. She explained that her cousin's wife couldn't conceive, and that as she, Carol Krusen, so enjoyed being pregnant, she agreed to carry the baby as a surrogacy. It's making me somewhat nauseous, she said, but nothing too terrible. Also, I'm studying to be a midwife and doula, so my life feels very integrated, like I've crossed a threshold back to where I always wanted to be.

Marie enjoyed Carol Krusen's updates, and didn't ask if, like other surrogates, Carol Krusen was being paid, or how much she could get if she decided to do it again. Neither did Marie talk much about her own life, except to share newsy information about her wife and stepchildren, and as she spoke, her accent and pauses became increasingly pronounced, so that Marie realized she was trying to make herself sound more like the people she had grown up with, like Carol Krusen and Marie's own siblings, who had stayed put. Why would that be, Marie later wondered, and is it possible to occupy two worlds simultaneously—home and away? And what if my idea of place blocks my ability to perceive? Because what is place but the matter and energy that exists there: people and plants, wind, dirt and rock, bumblebees and shifting bodies of water. And just as one tree can home hundreds of species, there are many inside of me. Marie decided she was onto something. Yes, she cried, you need to let a person and all their creatures be. Especially when she's your best friend, or your neighbor. Marie did not want Carol's life, even as Carol Krusen necessarily exceeded Marie's idea of who Marie wished she would be. And Marie's mother—she couldn't imagine Marie's desire as simply desire. Marie smiled then, knowing that her mother's imagination had nothing to do with her. Or she, for that matter, with her mother's desire.

It's strange how friends might help you without knowing that they do. Marie felt easier in life, and when she thought about Carol Krusen, she felt she understood Carol's gratefulness and freedom to be. And while Marie returned home with less frequency, she continued to receive updates about Carol Krusen, this time from her sister, Linda. For as these things happen, her sister's horrible neighbor, who had become, as these things also happen, her new best friend, was a midwife who had taken Carol Krusen on as an apprentice—a job for which she refused to be paid but was terrifically well-suited.

&

It was only later, after the moving truck came and left, that Marie understood the feeling beneath their adult voices.

Even later, Marie traced her finger from this spot on the mitten to that spot on the land above. A line just longer than her hand.

Late at night, Marie made a list of what to pack. Hike and hitch, she thought, and then came stories about dead girls found near lakes and streams. Too late for them, wept Marie. When she walked up the street to a new friend's house, she hid from passing cars.

Eventually, Marie quit dreaming that escape. Monette's house did not belong to Monette, either, she reasoned, and if you live in the woods, it's hard to reach the mall.

&

A Healthy Interest in the Lives of Others, Part II

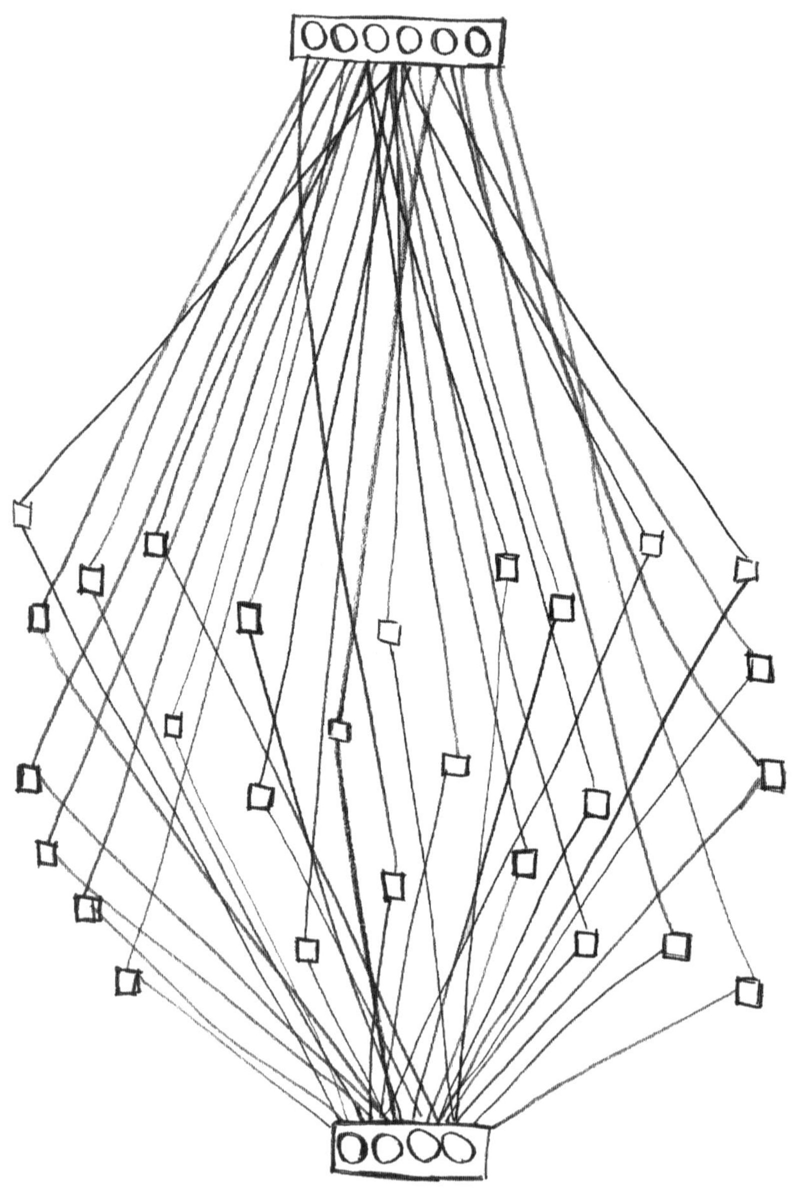

Before the panel, Angela had moved to the third row, choosing a chair not directly in front of her ex-best-friend, who, just as Angela predicted, had presented first. Angela refused to look at her, even when her ex-best-friend, it seemed anyway, tried to catch Angela's eye. During her talk, her ex-best-friend had said the same "writing is listening" line she'd been cooing since they'd met eight years prior, at the start of their MFAs. Now that they were no longer friends, Angela could imagine her ex-best-friend damning her with another of her favorite quips: *Angela quit listening.*

Angela literally rolled her eyes.

What is the writing that happens outside of writing? That was another of her ex-best-friend's favorite lines, and part of her quirky self-image was to film her own responses: walking, stirring cake batter, drawing a single purple line on a long sheet of paper. Angela hadn't clapped when her ex-best-friend finished her talk. She wasn't a hypocrite. She knew her ex-best-friend used to make fun of the poet (now a memoirist, too!) who spoke after her, but while this poet spoke, her ex-best-friend performed "listening." The poet (for that remained her primary identity) was chanting a list of animals. A small breeze moved through the room as the poet lifted her hands, prophet style, and proclaimed: "We! We! We! Are These!" Most everyone clapped and some snapped their fingers. Angela noticed the poet wore a combination of five different animal prints: cheetah, snake, zebra, leopard, cow. But no leather and certainly no fur. I like her, thought Angela, and although her ex-best-friend was already friendly with the poet, Angela determined to become her better friend. She would.

Animal Message: *There are no soft exchanges.*

Cathy snapped with just her right hand, barely raised, while almost smiling at the memoirist dressed in animal prints. She couldn't give the memoirist more than that. The room felt hot and a little too bright. Someone sitting close hadn't worn deodorant.

Before the panel, Cathy had introduced herself to the animal-printed poet, who had driven down from the Pacific Northwest. The poet asked Cathy about her work, and when Cathy used the phrase "creative services," the poet said that was such a corporate term. "It's like how we say 'languaged,'" continued the poet, "as in, how do you language that? Corporate America has turned language into a verb." Cathy couldn't decide if the poet was talking *at* or *past* her, so she widened her eyes and raised her eyebrows to see how the poet would respond. The poet leaned in and told Cathy she loved reading at art museums, and to keep her name in mind. Cathy had laughed just as Gina interrupted to say it was time to start and would the poet please take her seat in the front.

The problem, as Cathy saw it, was that the poet was too afraid to speak conclusive thoughts. Or rather, she was conflicted, because she wanted to say something urgent about the planet and its inhabitants, but she also wanted to be seen as an exceptionally intelligent human being who knew how to use obscuring language. Or, thought Cathy, maybe the poet's astrological chart is filled with more air signs than earth. Maybe she's all water and air, so her communication feels like a heartfelt spray, impossible to hold onto. Cathy continued to smile. She would complement the intellectual quality of the poet's talk. The poet would like that, thought Cathy, and there's a beautiful harmony, a service, really, in actively perceiving people as they want to be perceived.

As for herself, Cathy couldn't stand for people to not see her as caring, and thus went to great lengths to show how much she cared. She often gave presents, she called them surprises, little things she picked up here and there or made herself, like the three small succulents she'd grown from clippings and brought for Leon, Gina, and Niki. To thank them for organizing the event. She had placed the plants in the middle of the snack table, a nice bit of decoration among the water bottles and bowls of pretzels and nuts. They were, as Cathy hoped, an immediate conversation starter—with the animal-printed poet, yes, and before that with some sad slouching young man who had asked if she was William's friend before confessing that as William's former student, he had the biggest puppy-love crush on William and his writing.

"Is William coming?" the young sloucher had asked.

"No," said Cathy, with some alarm. "He's out of town."

The young sloucher, Cathy noticed, had seated himself in the row just behind her. For a moment, their eyes met. He waved. Cathy widened her eyes and tried to smile. *Oh no, oh William.*

On the panel, Marie began to speak.

Animal Message: *Friends lie.*

Angela closed her eyes for Marie's guided meditation.

"Imagine an animal," Marie said. "Don't overthink it. Let it be whatever animal wants to arrive." Angela saw a raccoon. Marie said to look at the animal and notice the feeling in your body. Angela's throat filled with nervousness, a stone of shame. Marie said to allow the animal to lead you to a memory. Angela returned to Piper, sitting across the table, avoiding Angela's eyes. That was Angela's first semester at art school, still so new to Southern California and, when people asked where she was from, she said her mother was French. But dead. Which awkwardly shifted the conversation. And Angela was realizing herself as bisexual, maybe even gay. She'd met Piper that first week of school and ran into her again one October weekend at a punk show. Piper was in a locally famous band, not the one playing that night, but Angela had seen Piper's image on posters hanging around campus and even in a cool record store on Sunset Boulevard. Angela was slightly surprised, then, when Piper remembered her and suggested they meet the following afternoon at a café so they could write together. Too late, Angela realized this had maybe been a date, which would explain the flushed feeling she couldn't name, because at that point in her life, Angela didn't know how to flirt with women and would regress to her middle school self, all awkward and strange. So, at the café, Angela was writing in her journal one minute and then, for reasons she still did not understand, she made circles with her index fingers and thumbs and held these to her eyes—as if she, Angela, were a raccoon, which was how she'd imagined herself—and she gazed at Piper through her finger-made frames while Piper began shifting uncomfortably in her seat. She had definitely freaked Piper out. A "serious weirdo." That's what Piper later called her, according to a mutual friend. Yes, thought Angela, she certainly was. But so was Angela's now ex-best-friend (don't let her name slip, no naming no), and the more serious Angela became about her writing, the more socially entwined she was with her cohort, including her ex-best friend, until Angela quit punk shows altogether for poetry readings. Angela discovered that she loved experimental writers. They were the punks of the literary scene—smart and socially awkward and generally stumbling in their small talk even as they wrote and broke rules on purpose. Many of them were slightly paranoid and self-obsessed. They liked words and had opinions about so many dead people and none of them felt like they had read enough of the right things, although all of them were ridiculously well read.

Animal Message: *Karmic reactions are inescapable.*

Leon and Frederick sat apart from the others, near the fan, in two chairs they'd pulled from the last row and placed near the door. Despite the fan's whir, Leon could hear Frederick's sharp inhalations, and for a moment the sound distracted him from the guided meditation and his own breath. Leon liked to jokingly call himself a "mindful failure," which annoyed some of his new-agey friends who warned him about self-talk and negativity. This amused Leon as he was far luckier and more laid-back than several of his so-called positive-thinking friends. Not that meditation wouldn't help him—Leon believed the science; he wasn't a fool. The brain is changeable, plastic, he wanted the neurological shifts. But his mind kept racing, it wasn't natural for his mind to be still. Trying to clear his mind, he thought, was like balancing a bicycle while standing still. Stop it and sit, he told himself. Focus on your breath. In and out and there was so much to do, he needed to ask Frederick about the story-essay. Part of Leon hoped Frederick would pass. The story-essay, Leon had decided, could be a big-seller, and if Leon published it himself, he could better market it and keep 100% of the profits. *We Have No Chance But to Use the Machine*—that's what Leon titled it. Leon was one of the few poets who didn't shy away from money and sales, which made him a good publisher of other people's poetry. That's where he'd put his energy for the past several years, and he enjoyed showing off what the community could do. Though sometimes, he missed the feeling of writing and had begun to worry, increasingly so, that his own practice was slipping away, so that by the time he returned to it, started his next big project, writing might not return to him. He didn't mention this to anyone but Frederick, who had very kindly invited him, a month or so later, to write a pamphlet that Frederick would publish. Frederick was so considerate that way. Nearby, Frederick sighed and tapped his foot. Dammit, Frederick. Leon took a deep breath and released. Frederick didn't like to talk about feelings and stuff like that. That's for writing, Frederick might say. So Leon wrote. The story-essay featured a cyborg bumblebee. It felt good.

Marie was presenting, something about dreams as a legitimate source of information. Leon was still friendly with Marie, even as she was on the outs with Frederick and a few others. Truth be told, he never got Marie. She used to curate a reading series, but every time she invited Leon to perform, he felt her prefatory disappointment, as if he were only there because her first choice had fallen through. Logically, he knew this wasn't the case; she always asked way before the publicity was generated and he performed too frequently for Marie to not respect his work. But there was some niggle there—maybe she didn't understand his writing and that's why they couldn't connect. Frederick thought Marie had a victim mentality, but Leon didn't get that feeling either. There wasn't enough of a charge between them for there to be an issue, maybe it was as simple as that.

Marie handed Leon two index cards. "For you," she smiled. "And Frederick."

Animal Message: *Distrust of apparent variation in someone.*

Joel played along with Marie's little writing game. It was an interesting approach to collaboration, but who knew if Marie was someone he'd want to be associated with, so no, he wasn't going to write his name. Also, it was a weird mix of animal stories. More about humans than animals, and there was something unsettling about them, though not in a necessarily interesting way. Because as they continued, Joel began to feel a strong sense of something unsaid. God, he hated that feeling, the creeping uncertainty and increasing tension. Mama's going off her rocker again, and Joel nearly groaned aloud. He hated thinking about his mother. He wanted Marie to stop.

And then he was down the rabbit hole, sitting with his older brothers and laughing as Mom threatened to check herself into Pine Rest, the mental home. She'd been saying that for years, and they'd started sassing back. "Over laundry?" they'd ask. "Over a messy room or a failed pot roast? Get a life, Mom," they would say. They sounded remarkably like their father, who'd been dead for many years. When Joel was in the eleventh grade, his mother did go to Pine Rest. She stayed for one month. His brothers were at college, so it was just him and his stepdad. They never mentioned his mother during her absence, and when she returned, she got the house back in order, even as there was a new vacancy about her. If anyone asked, she said she had been visiting her sister in Kansas City. She said this so frequently that Joel began to wonder if there was a sister he didn't know about. He finally asked. His mother laughed and said, "Maybe."

Animal Message: *We like to keep secrets, secret.*

It was time for a break. Marie tucked her papers into her bag and glanced at the bodies around her, some standing. Some turning around. She reached the bathroom queue just behind the poet, who didn't so much as glance at Marie, though they'd just paneled together. The poet was using her notebook to fan herself. Marie sighed and shifted her posture. Her back felt damp. She stood a little taller and said the poet's name.

"That was great," Marie said. Her voice sounded unusually high. The poet smiled with her mouth closed. "I especially liked the words for groups of nonhuman animals," continued Marie.

"Ah, yes," said the poet with a shrug. "Categorical foils."

"Okay," said Marie.

"The list is in my new book," said the poet, after a pause.

Marie nodded. "I'll have to check it out." When the poet didn't say anything, Marie continued, "The book's here, right?"

"Yeah," said the poet. She shuffled awkwardly and made a humming sound. "Okay," she said, "fifteen capitalist dollars." She rolled her eyes. "I would *gift* you a copy but I'm practicing self-care by valuing myself and my work. It's stupid how that means money, but I promised my therapist." She glanced toward the restroom door that was slowly opening. "It took over ten years to write," said the poet. "I mean, I wrote other things during that time, too."

"Oh no… I'll totally check it out," said Marie, who knew she would neither buy nor read the book. So why was she talking about it. God, sometimes she annoyed herself. The poet disappeared into the restroom. Marie sighed again. The poet wouldn't have spoken to her otherwise. Marie knew she had to talk first. About something the poet cared about. But there's nothing wrong with being nice to people, and she did like that list of words, even if it was copied from the internet.

Animal Message: *Reproduction is the ultimate stinging joke.*

Joel gravitated toward Niki without thinking. She was the attendee he was most familiar with, as they used to write for the same online indie blog. The site had been a big deal in its day, and a certain affinity still lingered among its writers. Niki greeted Joel pleasantly and introduced him to a dark-haired woman, Angela, who loudly complimented his writing. Joel shrugged and said the blog was a good time while it lasted. There was a sticky pause as no one mentioned the blog's founder, a well-known experimental fiction writer who had shut down the venue among allegations of sexual harassment and abuse from two or three women the blog founder had dated. They said he was not-unlike the rapey protagonists in his writing. Joel was pretty good friends with the blog's founder and thought the women were probably not-wrong in their allegations. He was a bit of a creep, his friend. But people like what they like, Joel had said while advising the blog's founder to please sit quiet and let it blow over, don't publish an open letter arguing that readers love these guys in fiction but have a boner-for-purity when it comes to "real" life. But the blog's founder prided himself on not shying away from controversy, so of course he published the letter, which included a paragraph naming his literary "fathers": Hemingway, Bukowski, Nabokov, Barthelme, Calvino. Tear those monuments down first, he wrote, with a slight hint that his detractors, especially his exes, mostly envied his success.

And then came the "Campaign for a Year Without Rape in Literature," which responded to far more than the blog founder's letter. There were signatures and circulated names, more debates and accusations—are we talking about rapey-authors or depictions of rape in general, and why only a year, and what is rape, and what's wrong with these women, and are they even women, because at a certain point, a conservative syndicated news and opinion site began covering what they called "the controversy," and their troll-y readers began filling the blog's comment sections with too many "Dumb Sluts" and other obvious and unoriginal insults for women, that at some point, the blog's founder gave up and shut the whole thing down.

See? Joel's friend wasn't a misogynist after all.

Joel hated those guys—the trollers. Evil orange–loving dittoheads who parroted their leaders' words while insisting they could think for themselves. When they first began commenting on the site, Joel had sometimes jumped in himself, just to ridicule and burn their asses. Fuck them sick fucks. They are literally making the whole world burn.

Animal Message: *We're the same as humans.*

By the time Cathy found Gina, she was surrounded by people Cathy did not know, including the slouching young man who liked William. Fans, that's what they seemed. Gina was telling a story about an artists' residency she'd been to that summer. The other residents, including a famous novelist, were afraid of mice, and as Gina was remarkably unsqueamish, and while she would have preferred a no-kill solution, she became the official mouse-catcher, she said, which really meant releasing dead mice from sprung traps and not looking too closely at their fine fur and perfectly formed paws, their wide heads and the nearly furless insides of their cute ears. Nothing like Mickey, she said.

The young sloucher guffawed, while Cathy and the others laughed nervously and looked away.

Everyone wanted to know what the famous novelist ate for lunch.

"Oh," said Gina with an expression of surprised remembering. "One of the residents knew you." Everyone turned toward Cathy, who brightened and widened her eyes.

"Caren Byrd," said Gina. "She said you set up a reading for her several years ago."

Cathy nodded vigorously and asked how Caren was, all the while trying to remember who Caren could possibly be.

Gina laughed and started talking about the famous novelist, who barely ate during the daylight hours. "He said he wrote better on an empty stomach but was a complete glutton after dark. He loved his gin and dry red wine. He had a thing for Caren, who was recently married and not giving it back." Gina laughed. "He's a bit of a dog." Gina paused. "Caren was his first choice, but he didn't waste time."

Everyone leaned in, Cathy included.

"No," laughed Gina again. "Honestly, he's kind of gross." She touched her neck and looked down, like she was trying to decide something. "Honestly," she said. "He wrote his number on my arm."

"And?" said the slouching young man.

Animal Message: *This is a human-animal message.*
It shuts out the ecological holism very much present.

Frederick experienced aggression. Marie sensed anger. Ana experienced anxiousness. Leon felt ashamed. Leon noticed bashfulness. Ana was touched with boredom. Marie noticed cautiousness. The poet felt confidence. Joel experienced confusion. Niki noticed curiosity. Niki had depression. Joel sensed determination. Angela suffered disappointment. Angela held disbelief. Frederick suffered disgust. The poet sensed ecstasy. Gina perceived embarrassment. The poet experienced rage. Ana suffered envy. Niki perceived exasperation. Gina suffered exhaustion. Frederick was touched with fear. Niki was aware of frustration. Leon perceived grief. Marie felt guilty. Frederick held happiness. Gina was aware of hope. Leon suffered hurt. Joel noticed indifference. Niki sensed interest. Ana suffered jealousy. Angela sensed joy. Marie perceived kindness. Frederick felt knowledgeable. Gina sensed kookiness. Gina was touched with loneliness. Niki noticed love. The poet sensed lovingness. Cathy felt miserable. Leon experienced numbness. The poet suffered neglect. Cathy experienced optimism. Leon was aware of the overwhelm. Frederick felt pain. Joel experienced puzzlement. Marie experienced queasiness. The poet noticed querulousness. Leon experienced regret. Joel experienced relief. Joel noticed sadness. Marie was touched with satisfaction. Gina experienced shock. Cathy held shyness. Gina noticed smugness. Frederick felt sorry. The poet experienced stubbornness. Joel was aware of stupidity. Ana felt surprised. Leon experienced suspicion. Cathy perceived thoughtfulness. Leon was aware of upset. Frederick felt uncomfortable. Niki was touched with value. Marie noticed withdrawal. Cathy felt xenial. Gina sensed yucky. Angela perceived yearning. Joel suffered zealousness. The poet experienced zest.

Animal Message: *You can't control the outcome of your genuine nature.*

Leon found Frederick talking with Ana Falu near the snack table. The two of them had become quite the collaborators, so much so that for a while it seemed they were dating, a suggestion they often greeted with a sly smile. Those who were closer to Ana, like Leon, knew she was asexual.

"Oh, hello," said Ana, making room at the table.

"What's going on?" Leon said. He leaned forward to grab a handful of pretzels from a green bowl.

"We were talking about Marie's presentation," said Ana.

"The great enlightenment meets co-opted labor," added Frederick. He and Ana laughed while Leon shrugged. He was less sensitive, he guessed.

There was an awkward pause.

"Hey," said Leon with a sudden glow. "Great talk."

"Thanks, Leon." Ana's voice was low and clear.

"Tuning in, tuning in," said Frederick. Leon and Ana waited as Frederick slowly nodded his head. "Maybe this will be our last *Be Papered*," he said, "you know everything has its time."

"Oh!" said Ana, catching sight of someone in the other room. "I have to go, but Frederick, things happen." She smiled and patted his shoulder.

Leon watched her walk away. He felt disappointed.

Frederick began humming a Marx Brothers song.

Leon took another handful of pretzels.

"So," said Frederick, crossing his arms over her chest. "How about January for your pamphlet?"

Leon frowned and nodded.

Animal Message: *Maternity and survival are mutually exclusive in the forging of friendship.*

Cathy stepped outside and opened a search browser on her phone. Caren Bryd slowly became familiar. Years ago, when Cathy's initial reading series was just gaining traction, poets she didn't know began contacting her for readings in the city, and Caren Byrd was one of these. Cathy had set up a Sunday afternoon event for Caren and her friend, another white woman, at one of the trendier bookstores. Cathy wasn't sure why she agreed to their request, except for her familiar sense of obligation—she had a habit of imagining herself asking for help, then giving the response she'd want to hear—so she said yes and asked for copies of their books. Cathy can't remember anything about the poems except that they were lyrical with line breaks and just long enough to fit one poem per page. Reading them, she'd felt slightly thirsty. Still, she introduced the poets by talking about the beautiful necessity of their words and even used the breathy tone poets prefer for flattering each other. Afterward, the two poets thanked Cathy and left with some local friends for dinner at a nearby restaurant. They didn't invite Cathy to join them. Or send a thank you or offer to host a reading if Cathy came to their east coast town. Cathy organized events because she believed that stories and poems are the webs that weave us together. This happens with the stories we tell ourselves, too.

Animal Message: *Without an understanding of context, hypocrisy and sincerity can seem twins.*

To be clear: Marie didn't consider the poet to be a bad writer of a bad book. What is a bad book, anyway? It's much healthier to focus on what moves us, so another way to say this is: Marie wouldn't read the poet's memoir because she didn't like it enough to want it on her shelf, and her shelves were already filled with books she still wanted to read. As Marie didn't identify as a poet, she rarely felt compelled to do more than attend poets' readings, where she would hear enough to gain a general sense of their writing. Marie hoped the poet would understand: she was glad for her poems railing against oppressive social structures and the devaluing of non-human species. You can be glad for someone even as you don't want to be their friend or read their books.

On the panel, someone had mentioned a story written by one of Marie's ex-friends, and as Marie washed her hands, she glanced uneasily at her own reflection. To her closer friends, Marie said that this ex-friend's choice of a husband had marked the beginning of their friendship's end. Sometimes, Marie would list the husband's pluses and minuses, while assuring her listener that the ex-friend was as manipulative as she was manipulated. Marie had examples. She'd discovered them the weekend of the wedding. Hosted at a lodge in the mountains, Marie had shared a room with two other friends and all three women thought the bride was making a mistake. What did she see in him? All weekend, the friends compared notes and stories, until their tongues had shaped the bride into a monster (to be fair, she'd already had an affair, as humans sometimes do), though they'd smiled for the cameras, and hugged the bride, and were, in effect, horribly fake. Which was, of course, their judgment of her. "I'm sorry," mouthed Marie, as she closed her eyes and imagined the face of her ex-friend, who wasn't at *Be Papered*, who had, in fact, sold her last two books, including the story mentioned on the panel, to one of the big five publishers—another reason she was out of step with this particular crowd.

Animal Message: *The fact that more than we think is true doesn't preclude friendship.*

Joel stepped outside just as Niki began circulating with a five-minute notice. The air was hot; he squinted in the too-bright sun. He wanted the beef jerky he'd stashed in his glove compartment and wanted to eat it in peace. An amorphous "they" used to accuse the blog of being a boys club, but the cliquishness of the *Be Papered* set made him feel like the boys' blog had a brightly colored welcome mat at its virtual door. The conversation with Niki and that other woman had been nothing more than awkward, though he saw their faces brighten when Frederick said hello. The car was warm; he took a bite of jerky and relaxed into its salty greasiness. "So delicious," he said aloud. He flipped down the car visor and pushed open the mirror cover. He liked to watch himself chew. It wasn't a particularly pleasant image; that's what he liked about it. He could taste more of the meat. His teeth looked too small for his head. When he was younger, he used to eat tuna sandwiches in front of the bathroom mirror and that's when he discovered how difficult it was to contain your own spit while chewing with your mouth open. His mother chewed with her mouth open, even when others were present.

Frederick, he'd decided, was a pompous ass. Frederick had greeted Niki and the other woman with an exaggerated wave, but barely glanced at Joel, who'd introduced himself nonetheless.

"We share a publisher," said Joel, in case Frederick didn't recognize him. "I really liked your last book."

"Thanks," said Frederick. And after a pause, "Connections, connections," as if that's all Joel cared about.

Joel had gone a bit foggy. He shrugged, "Okay," and tilted his head to get a better look at Frederick, who was shorter than Joel had imagined.

"I'd heard you moved to town," said Frederick.

Joel had nodded. Everyone felt uncomfortable.

Frederick turned toward Niki and the other woman and began making empty comments about the afternoon.

Joel listened.

It became clear from their talking that most of them, including the speakers, had gone to the same art school. Had even, in many cases, been in the same cohort or class. How boring, thought Joel. No wonder the panel had felt like a circle of back-patters, as opposed to a circle jerk. This crowd was too tame to bare their genitals.

At the blog, they'd at least tried to engage strangers. They weren't open to unsolicited submissions, that was true, but they were serious about the conversation in the comments area. If someone wanted to challenge, learn more, offer another perspective—they were all in for a rigorous discussion, dissent welcomed. That was the ethos of the now-tainted founder, and at its peak, their comments section had been full of arguments, blusterings, affections, and of course the occasional troll. They were annoying, yes, but Joel was suspicious of public displays of piety, too, which is why he had refused to sign the "Campaign for a Year Without Rape in Literature" and another open letter that began circulating shortly thereafter, advocating for freedom of speech while also denouncing a number of rapey-men, including the founder, his friend. *We are*, wrote the letter writers, *refusing binary thinking.*

Niki signed that one. She also sent a personal email to Joel, confessing a feeling of *have to*, she couldn't explain why. She had written to Joel, he knew, because he was the person who initially hooked her into the group as a featured writer. For a minute, Joel had thought about publishing the email as proof of female hypocrisy; then again, what would that prove? That women are entitled to be human, too?

Frederick, Joel realized, didn't want Niki and that other woman to think that he, Frederick, was sexist.

"What a cowardly ass," said Joel, looking himself in the eye.

Animal Message: *To bury awareness is an unattractive personality flaw.*

The second panel began and Leon tuned out almost immediately—the first speaker was mumbling about something he was going to say but wasn't saying yet. And Leon needed to think about this Frederick situation, if he should go ahead and let Frederick publish his story-essay. Frederick had been very enthusiastic, calling it his favorite of Leon's writings. Leon knew the story-essay was very good. He'd felt a thrilling hum while composing, a sense that, with the right positioning, it could become something more. Something big. Maybe giving it to Frederick was a waste. Because Frederick would publish a small edition of only 100 copies, priced at $7 each, as that was his standard practice, and this suddenly felt like damning the story-essay to an early grave. There was no money in pamphlets, especially when at least 30 of the 100 copies would be given away as promos. Because the point was for others—the right others—to read the writing and to want to help the writer publish more. That was the promise of the pamphlets.

But Leon believed his story-essay was worth some money. Or it could be. With the right frame. The well-positioned platform.

The room paused as Gina turned off the overhead lights. The speaker had a slideshow of poems he'd installed throughout the city. Sometimes the poems stayed wheat-pasted up; other times they washed away with the tide or wind or an intervention from a passerby. It wasn't a new idea and the poems were decent enough, certainly clever, so Leon was surprised that he was so annoyed, even angry. There was something sanctimonious in the speaker's voice, like this was real poetry because it wasn't for sale, when the fact is, thought Leon, you can make money from art. You just need to know your niche, your market. Money itself, thought Leon, is neutral. Like nature and machines.

Animal Message: *Patience, generosity, and the ability to be harmonious are possible when you can't see the unexpected gifts of life coming.*

Angela looked at the poet's email address, written on a sticky note in purple pen and carefully placed on the title page of her book. The poet's handwriting was fabulously loopy. Angela smiled. They'd had a nice conversation, and when Angela mentioned that her first book was coming out next spring, the poet invited her to read in her city, and to stay with her, too. Angela had always wanted to visit Portland. Yes, she would definitely make the trip.

Angela closed the poet's book to listen to Cathy, who was just beginning to speak. She enjoyed Cathy's enthusiasm, though she had to admit it was an acquired taste. Cathy was so bubbly, so relentlessly positive, that for the longest time, Angela couldn't believe it wasn't an act. Angela and her ex-best-friend used to refer to Cathy as "our punctured

Polyanna," for while Angela and her ex-best-friend didn't know the details of Cathy's childhood, they assumed she'd suffered all sorts of trauma, as is bound to be the case with someone—like Cathy, like Angela, like her ex-best friend—who doesn't fit the culture's idea of "normal." Cathy was saying that poetry already exists all around us, so there isn't an *unexpected* place to bring it. Rather, we need to embrace our own openness, see ourselves as language, that when we bring two unlikes together, we've entered the poetic frame of mind. And made those parts of us more visible.

Angela turned to see her ex-best-friend (Ana, okay she'll name her), and something drained away—a tightness or a position. A fear. Cathy was talking again, saying the word *activist, activist* in her ever-upbeat pitch, and Angela glanced again at Ana, who was sitting so erect and at attention, so stone-faced still that Angela could see something just beneath the surface. She's proud of herself, thought Angela, and before she could move fully into the next logical question, she realized its answer. Ana felt triumphant in her "boundary-setting," that's the term she would use to describe it. Ana was doing what she needed to protect herself from an emotionally suffocating monster. Angela felt a keening sadness well up within her.

Oh, thought Angela, that monstrous me.

Animal Message: *You don't love me, I won't talk to you.*

Cathy stood in front of the crowd, not talking but peering with a certain measure of intensity and not quite a smile on her face. Somebody sneezed. "Gesundheit," she said. To her right, a man laughed while on the other side of the room came the sound of an escaped sob. She started her phone's timer for sixty-eight seconds and looked in that direction, breathing into her heart's center. The space began to feel longer, bigger, as she gazed, one by one at every face in the room. So many agreed to her unspoken instructions, their eyes meeting hers, though what she read there shifted with their postures, their level of shared familiarity, the almost visible voices in their heads. This one wanted approval, was trying to please her. This one didn't reveal but didn't look away. These ones refused, allowed themselves to be distracted, yawned in ambivalence. These ones wondered what would happen, got bored, closed their eyes, followed her gaze as it moved through the room. Cathy could hear the other panelists sniff and shift in their seats.

Cathy's phone trilled harp sounds. She turned it off before pushing aside her prepared remarks.

She smiled again, bright and calm. "In conclusion," she said: "There was once a girl who kept a table with only three legs. I say only, because in the corner where the fourth leg should have been, there was nothing but air. Because this was not a nice three-legged table, designed with an equilateral triangle extending from its center. Rather, this table was made from necessity and life, from what happens with wear and the wearying years. The girl wasn't very old. She'd just gotten her period for the first time, a relief because if anyone were to ask, which no one probably would, she could finally say yes. She menstruated! The girl referred to her table as a platform, especially when speaking to her dog, a small black terrier called Chalmette."

Cathy paused, pressed her lips together, swallowed. "The girl used her table or platform for all sorts of activities. Painting and writing letters. Eating and playing solitaire. For as long as it was the girl who sat at the table, and not someone like her sighing mother or slightly older cousin with bad breath, the table with the three legs magically stayed upright and stable, available for her use."

Cathy paused again to gather her papers. She peered at nothing.

"My question," she said, "is simple: What makes this girl's three-legged table stand?"

Animal Message: *I want it both ways—always.*

Joel didn't return to *Be Papered*. It was lame, he decided, but if he went in and said this to anyone they'd accuse him of being ableist and end the conversation there. He probably was. Because wasn't that common knowledge: that if you live in an ableist, and racist, and sexist, and homophobic society, then you're that too? Stands to reason, and he was happy he could think.

Joel wished things could go back to how they were, when writing conversations were about writing and not a constant performance of virtue-signaling. Dwelling on your shortcomings made them worse, he thought, and if you're convinced you won't amount to much, you won't. Most of the *Be Papered* writers were better people than poets, so maybe they should work on that.

He turned on his car and checked his phone. His wife had texted about dinner. He sent her a "thumbs up," and thought for a moment about which store would be best for sweet onions, flat bread, and cheap wine. Last week, he'd been talking at the bookstore about his wife when his co-worker stopped him to say, "Your wife, your wife, she has a name. What is it?"

"Miranda," he'd shot back, but his hot flash of defensiveness quickly passed as his co-worker smiled. "The *warning* is your *right*."

Animal Message: *Don't feed us like pigs!*

Leon decided to email Frederick but first needed a few beers, beginning with one from Gina because he'd won the bet about Juli. She'd sent an apology about sadly missing *Be Papered* since it coincided with her bicycle-activist-artist event, where she was a key presenter. "Classic Juli," Leon said to Gina, who seemed to agree, or at least didn't argue.

Leon opened another beer and reviewed his plan. He'd tell Frederick that he wanted to self-publish the story-essay as part of a new small paperback series called *Experiment: West Coast*. Frederick should send him a piece for the series, or Frederick could collaborate with Ana Falu, whatever he wanted. Leon would explain that his story-essay was a manifesto for the series—that's why he needed to publish it, rather than Frederick, he hoped Frederick would understand.

Leon felt pleased with himself.

Why edit an anthology when he could publish an unbound series of West Coast writers, and people like Juli can't or won't get mad about who's included because doing so might spoil their chance of making it in. It's good to cover all bases.

Animal Message: *Family dinners are really awful for animals too.*

That night, Angela dreamt or read about raccoons. They aren't as solitary as people think; some even say they're homosocial. The males often live with unrelated males in stable groups of four or less, while females live in what is known as fission-fusion societies, splitting apart and coming back together depending on the activity and the season, so the size of the group changes. Meaning change is their stable factor. Angela could not understand herself as a danger, the one from whom Ana needed protection. In her dream or in the book, the raccoon was hungry or tired and searching for something to eat or for a place to nest. Or curious about that strange new smell. In her dream or in the book, the raccoon wanted to play—when she turned around, there were other raccoons near the tree. Raccoon approached the nearest one and tapped it with her right paw. The tapped raccoon released a high-pitched whistle and another raccoon appeared, larger, grunting. Angela smelt the alpha; she didn't want to fight. In her dream or in the book, the raccoon ran down a path toward the hoot of an owl. Or the sound of an other-worldly creature. Animal-us.

When she woke or quit reading, Angela began drawing a raccoon in her notebook. RACCOON, she wrote beside her drawing, which looked, yes, a bit cartoonish. With a purple pencil, she colored in its mask. Cartoons are fine, she decided.

Animal Message: *Found agreement with another's narrative.*

The morning after the event, Marie walked with her dogs around the neighborhood. She had thought community meant belonging, but this morning the word *vulnerability* rang in her ears. Every animal must navigate the possibility of harm. Worms and moles dig underground tunnels, and rabbits generally wait for nightfall before leaving their nests. Bees will swarm a predatory wasp, while chameleons fade into their backgrounds. For monkeys, the group is the protection, just like there's protection in being the top gorilla or submitting to the alpha. Humans gossip, project images, try to control how others see them. They attack, get busy or buy houses, focus on saving or spending money while calling each other variations of *good* or *bad*, *best friend* or *wife*.

In front of the house, Marie squatted and the dogs turned toward her, pressing their heads into her body as she rubbed one's belly, the other's neck.

They breathed together, sensing an ache and inner thrum. A quickening.

Above her, the hot sky filled with smoke.

Animal Message: *You can force anything to believe in regimentation.*

&

That night the moon glowed crescent gold with one star visible below it.

Inside, Marie lit a candle.

If she saw Monette, would she know her?

If she smelled her, would she let her go?

&

My Dear Unfriend

a story works toward a sentence

In her email, Michele wrote that while she was willing to talk with Marie in person, she would not be available until after June sixteenth. The matter at hand was their friendship; the email was dated April tenth. "Okay," said Marie to the blue-lit screen. "I guess you are upset with me." A familiar chill filled Marie's body. She hadn't spoken with Michele for several months, that was true, but the two women rarely saw each other these days so Marie hadn't registered Michele's silence as unusually strange. But three days ago, when Michele still had not responded to either of Marie's invitations—an email sent in mid-March, a text a week later—asking if she would like to go see their former teacher, Kevin, read at a queer literary event, Marie decided to check Michele's social media accounts. Maybe Michele was sick! Or caught in some flame-war or other posturing flurry! Online, Marie found that Michele, who she had known now for nearly two decades, who had been her BFF before a friendship break that took years to mend, and while things weren't the same—how could they be—the two women feeling their way into this new, more mature friendship, that's what Marie thought, anyway, until—Marie found that Michele had unfriended her.

"Time makes us grow, atrophy, ferment…. Anything else?" asked Marie. "Rot," suggested Michele with a laugh. That was the previous August, one of the last times they'd seen each other in person, at Michele's house for what Marie had learned, that day, was an annual BBQ. Michele had texted an invite to Marie just the day before. Marie came late, lingered until the other guests left. Michele's partner, Rocky, had uncorked another bottle of wine before taking the dog for a walk. Michele and Marie toasted Michele's forthcoming book, this one published by an even larger indie-press with a solid national reputation. Yes, Marie would be at the launch event in October. "You're in it," smiled Michele. "I have a story about you, too," said Marie. She removed her sunglasses, fussed her hair-bun. "But listen…" Marie wanted to confide in Michele. She began with the easies and likely-knowns, like how Marie had been dropped by a small group of mutual friends, which hurt, yes, but also gave space to reevaluate her friendships. "You know them," said Marie, "all straight, white, and vegan." She paused while Michele gave a funny laugh. Marie had worried that the vegans might be at Michele's BBQ—this was Los Angeles, there were always vegan options—but neither woman mentioned their absence. The women didn't comment on the complicated history of their own friendship, either. "But Michele," said Marie, "I have more serious news." She'd been diagnosed with breast cancer. Very early stage. Left breast. Right above the heart. She had already undergone two surgeries and would begin six weeks of radiation therapy right before her birthday. But the prognosis was so positive, she reassured, that she could approach the illness as a meditation on her own mortality, albeit in a deep and visceral way. "After all," she smiled, "we're writers." At the mention of cancer, Michele became teary, which surprised

Marie almost as much as the flashed insight which followed: that Michele was feeling into the reality of her own frailty. Marie could nearly hear her later that evening, whispering to Rocky about the strange poignancy of aging, how friends get sick. Die, even. At least Michele did not to say this aloud to Marie, did not, in other words, turn Marie's illness into a poem imagining herself as ill. That's progress, thought Marie, who smiled at Michele with genuine fondness and accepted her tears as a small offering to their friendship. As she was leaving, Marie promised to call if she needed anything, but knew she wouldn't. Because even though Marie's wife, Louise, was moving ahead with a planned five-week trip to Paris—Louise insisted she needed it, "you'll be fine," she told Marie—Marie had other, closer friends, who would stay with her during the most tiring weeks of radiation.

As much as Marie could remember, the two women had never been honest with each other about their friendship. Even in their rekindled connection, they had agreed to "let bygones be water under that big ass bridge now behind them." Clichés, they decided, were sometimes unavoidable. Or easier, Marie thought, as she recalled a more uncomfortable conversation they'd had during their third year of friendship when Michele "needed space" and things had gotten weird and constantly subtextual. At that time, Marie was actively realizing her queerness while Michele was going through another "I want dick" phase. But their first two years of friendship—oh that time was glorious! At least to Marie, who in her mid-twenties had become so accustomed to the stone-ache of loneliness she often dreamt herself lost in an overgrown yet dying forest, panicked when she could not sense the blue-sky above or the brown-earth beneath.

So, when she met Michele in a writing workshop, she felt as if she had finally found a clearing in those woods; the sun shone, everything was brighter, the shadows slipped away. By the end of summer, the two women were speaking on the phone at least once, though usually two or three times a day, and seeing each other weekly, if not more. They both had boyfriends but had dated women. They identified as "non-identified." "I want a sexual charge in all my relationships," sighed Michele. Marie nodded, and wondered if that meant Michele's friendships, too. More than anything, they wanted to be writers. Artists. To conjure worlds with words. That year, they applied to the same low-residency MFA program. When they were accepted, they compared notes about the phone call they'd received from the same faculty member—a published and, to them anyway, famous author. "Dennis said he was personally very impressed with my writing," said Michele, and Marie wished she could remember exactly what Dennis had said to her. But she had answered the call while on the toilet, was stuck there, unable to take notes or wipe or flush as Dennis said something about her "interesting" application. She absolutely remembered that word. The whole situation provided a good story, one that made Michele laugh. And Marie liked to make Michele laugh. She liked to praise her writing, too, which she genuinely admired. It felt good to compliment Michele, and fawning was one of Marie's familiar safeties, so instinctual she didn't realize the soothed feelings it produced weren't her own. This, then, had been their initial dynamic; but by their third year of friendship, they had grown weary of it and each other. Or maybe it was just Marie, who tired of being the self-appointed sidekick. Why couldn't she believe in herself like she believed in Michele? That was when Marie's father died, suddenly and not yet sixty. While Marie traveled to Michigan to bury him and mourn, Michele wrote poems about how she would feel if her father died, which she posted in their virtual MFA workshop. Marie read the poems with perplexed horror. She was sitting in her parents' bedroom, having used their old computer and dial-up internet to log into the workshop, all too aware that her father's heart had quit beating while he was lying on the bed behind her, the one still covered in the pink and blue rose-pattern comforter that had covered him. Nearby, in a child-sized green rocking chair, sat the large stuffed raccoon she'd received for her tenth birthday. "Hey you," she said to the animal. "You saw him die."

The event, Kevin's reading, was billed as part of a week-long festival of queer writing. Marie was almost glad that Louise was out of town, as she would have scoffed at what she called "the more conservative literary aesthetic of the more popular gays." Marie did not disagree—legibility does lubricate sales—but she also wondered about the politics of envy and how being left out and looked over tainted one's critique. Parking that evening, Marie flashed on her ex-friends, the straight, white vegans and their super-experimental writing, and then on Michele, her new unfriend, whose third book was gathering prominent reviews—as was Kevin's new memoir about his friendship with another writer, a cis-het straight woman now dead from cancer. Marie knew about a glowing *Times* review from social media but had not otherwise kept in contact with Kevin and did not know how he would receive her. She would not disclose her own cancer, even though experience had sharpened her awareness of mortality and what matters, was a main reason she wanted to… reconnect. Yes, that was it. Marie would have gone to Kevin's reading even if his book hadn't received fancy reviews or, like Marie's latest book, only one review on a janky lit blog with ugly colors and bad formatting. Readers, Marie often told her students, don't owe you anything, so it's best to be grateful for anyone's attention to your work. Kevin had just started his performance when Marie entered the multipurpose, fluorescent-lit meeting room, converted that night into an auditorium. She slipped into the last row and relaxed into his reading, the pacing and breath of his sentences, his particular enunciation, melodious and full and slightly more from the right side of his mouth. As her first real writing teacher, she had studied him with that peculiar mixture of hunger and fascination that young artists often have for their mentors. She sees this now, though at the time, and for many years after, she couldn't admit how much she wanted to be at the podium, reading from her own book, freshly published, smartly designed. "I'd rather write artistically excellent books than be famous," said Michele, shortly before their MFA graduation. Marie had insisted that Michele would not have to choose. "Just wait until you're up there," Marie would say. "I can see you, powerfully holding the room." Marie wanted Michele to speak this vision for Marie. "Yes," said Michele. "I can see me, too."

Two or ten minutes into Kevin's reading about his complicated relationship with another writer, Marie began to worry-fantasize about Michele. She scanned the crowd but did not see her. Would Michele even go, knowing Marie might attend? Well, if she did, Marie would ask her, point blank, if she had unfriended Marie because of The Story. It was a piece Marie had written a few years prior, while staying at an artists' colony in the Northeast. At the time, she and Michele were no longer actively ignoring each other in public, but they weren't on each other's party-invite lists either, and they certainly weren't getting together, just the two of them. The Story was about the first few months of their friendship. It had risen from its first sentence, the way stories sometimes do, with such a swirl of energy that when it was finished Marie walked into the nearby woods, weeping and watching the squirrels as they ran for cover or froze halfway up various kinds of trees. She was, she realized, ready to see Michele, to give their friendship another go. Michele had already expressed this desire, apologizing over email for not being there when Marie had come out to her mother and fallen in love with Louise—it happened so fast, within eighteen months of Marie's father's death. *When I fell in love with Rocky*, wrote Michele, *I wanted someone to talk to, and realized you must have wanted someone, too.* At the time, Marie had thanked Michele for her apology, but wasn't ready for renewed friendship. Writing The Story, however, did something to Marie's insides, made what had been painful into something okay. So, when she returned from the Northeast, she reached out to Michele, and the two women began meeting again for the occasional coffee or drink. Two or three times, including at the BBQ in August, Marie mentioned The Story, but Michele never asked to see it and Marie didn't share it until after it was published, just that past December in an online journal. Marie emailed the link to Michele that same day with a note that read: "You may find this amusing, or you may hate it." Michele wrote back a few hours later, a one-sentence response: *Thank you for sending this*. Now it was April and Michele had unfriended her. Michele, said Marie in her imaginary conversation, The Story is fiction, an exaggeration, less about you and more about writing and what happens when you consciously allow language to deform, and thus recreate, your life.

Women tend to write about characters and interpersonal relationships, while men focus on action and external change, and this exacerbates issues of inequality because the publishing industry rewards plot-driven books. This was one of the several issues people argued about in Marie's MFA program, and because, at that point, Marie wasn't thinking about publication, she focused on the first part of that statement: Was it true that women emphasized character over plot? Her own relationships were filled with so many twists and turns that she didn't see how it was possible to separate one from another—the action from the character, the language used from the person made through speech. Or by not speaking but stewing about it, which Marie sometimes chose. It had taken her over a year, for example, to confront Michele for posting poems about her father's imaginary death, knowing, as she must have, that Marie would see the poems days after burying her own father. Marie had brought it up—finally!—during the conversation Michele had initiated about needing "more space." In her defense, Michele said she had assumed Marie would be so consumed with grief she wouldn't bother logging into the workshop discussion. But Marie did, of course, and not only because their teacher insisted that Marie continue to write despite and through the grief, but because the conversation about writing, about something other than funerals and flowers, provided some relief. Still, her father's death marked the beginning of their friendship's first ending, so by the time he'd been gone for two years, Marie and Michele were no longer speaking.

Nurtured. That's a word Kevin used to describe his relationship with his now-dead friend. He also spoke of feeling beleaguered, weary, in love, competitive, silenced, guilty, compassionate. He didn't use those words exactly, but such conflicting emotions and sensibilities swirled throughout his reading—a scene from when they first met, another from several years into their friendship during one of his friend's many love dramas. As he read, Marie studied his olive-green newsboy cap, wondering about its personal significance and if there was an image he stepped into when he put it on. She and Michele used to joke about their writing hats—Marie's was a colorful faux-fur Russian ushanka while Michele had a cowboy hat made of straw. Put that hat on and get to writing, they would tease each other, though they rarely spoke about why they might need the hats. The one-time Marie confessed her sometimes-guilty feeling about being in a MFA program—maybe she didn't belong there, maybe someone more deserving should have her space—Michele only sighed and suggested that Marie talk to a therapist. Marie had wanted sympathy, validation, maybe a few compliments about her writing, but these were things that Michele instinctively, knowingly, withheld. People give the most compliments right before they ask a question, noted Marie, as Kevin's reading ended and the event turned into a familiar Q&A with remarks about the book's form, its title, what Kevin was working on now. Michele wasn't there and Marie realized how ridiculous she'd been to imagine she might be, but Marie did see Dennis, the former MFA faculty member who'd called them so long ago. After the Q&A, he and Marie greeted each other warmly. "How is Michele," he asked. Marie smiled, shrugged. "Don't know," she said. And then, because it was awkward, "but I was at her book release." Dennis smiled. He was sorry to miss it. "What are you working on?" he asked. "Stories," said Marie. She paused. "About writing and gossip." She told him the collection's title and he laughed. "Can't wait," he said. "Let me know if I can help." The look on Marie's face prompted him to continue. "I know we never worked together," he said, "but yours is one of the few applications I remember… that ribbon of ants walking across your bedroom wall." Marie flushed. Yes, she remembered. She called their trail Highway 61.

"Internal realities, like, they do create our worlds?" Marie sidled up to Kevin, who smiled and moved to make room for her in the group. The speaker was a young man with shaggy hair, likely a student, maybe gay, it was hard for Marie to tell. "I mean, did writing this," the man continued, "help you to understand more about your friendship?" Kevin smiled and nodded. "Sure," he said, with a pause. "But that's not why I wrote it." The young man slightly squinted as Kevin turned toward Marie. "Hello," he said. "Gosh, thanks for coming." "I enjoyed your reading." "Oh, wow, thanks, you look well." As they spoke, the young man played with a brightly colored pencil, tapping it against his knuckles as he glanced from Marie to Kevin to the people around them and back. At the first pause in Kevin and Marie's conversation, he tugged a little at Kevin's sleeve. "Did you always want to write about her?" "Oh, heavens no," said Kevin, turning more fully toward the young man. "But we were very good friends."

Visions come to those who ask, thought Marie the next day. She was reading a notebook from her twenties, when she still called Michele her best friend. How she had loved Michele, her confidence and charisma, the way she braided her hair, her steely look and elevated posture when she asked a difficult or challenging question. But it was also complicated. She remembered Michele talking and talking about her amazing writing, how well it was going, while Marie's notebook was mostly "morning pages," an exercise from Julia Cameron's *The Artist's Way*. How frequently Marie's pages filled with frets about Michele! How convinced Marie was that if she spoke too much, shined too much, or wrote something that earned the praise of others, Michele would sever the relationship. Or, in the very least, would call Marie petty, catty, and superficial, which is how she summarized two older female classmates after—and this was the key— the four of them had dinner one night, and the two other women spoke more to Marie, were more interested in her writing. And yes, the women were petty and catty. But they were also being honest. "The more I like what I am writing," read Marie in one old notebook, "the more silent Michele's response." Years later, when Marie and Michele began their slow dance of reconciliation, they gestured interest in each other's work. Michele posted Marie's book on social media and Marie bought Michele's book and asked her to sign it. But they never talked about the actual content, maybe out of mutual respect and their desire to rebuild a friendship, or maybe because of their old competitiveness, which remained undiscussed. Around that time, too, Michele sent Marie a Facebook message with a link to a poem she'd published. *You'll understand when you read it*, she wrote, and Marie did, though her understanding differed, quite likely, from what Michele imagined. The poem was addressed to an erotic *you* and included a series of evocative images from places and experiences they had shared. It was written to amplify sexual tension between them, and framed as a relationship-spell that Michele broke when she fell in love with her first girl-friend. It was, remembered Marie, exactly as Michele would need to see it, and she hadn't envied Michele that need or the poem. Marie still considered Michele a good writer, but realized she wasn't interested in making the kinds of things that Michele made. What a relief! Because for so long, she had held Michele as the real writer, the one she needed to emulate or push forward, the one whose success felt like a necessary safety to Marie's own.

Their sticky situation reminded Marie of something the writer Yxta Maya Murray once said: that all writing—and Marie wondered if *writing* included relationships, with their scripted plays we try and sometimes do disrupt—could be distilled to either: "Fuck you, Mama" or "Mama, do you love me now?"

Friendship is something you repeatedly choose and Marie's investigation into Michele's unfriending was far from over. She called her friend Monica first, also a writer and some-one Marie trusted to answer truthfully: What wasn't Marie seeing? Was The Story actually, as one editor suggested, gratuitously mean? No, Monica didn't think so, she loved The Story, and people love to call female writers "mean." Yet it's often difficult, Monica continued, for people to read themselves in fiction. She told Marie about her own high school friend, and how upset she'd been when Monica wrote a story with a character based on her. "It was painful," said Monica, "for my friend to revisit that period of our lives. I did it consciously; I wrote it. But for her, the story felt like a slap from nowhere. Though she got it, too, that the story wasn't her, or us—it's its own thing. Art." Marie nodded. She thought about how she appeared in Michele's writing—not as herself, but as Michele's idea of Marie. And Michele's need to romanticize herself. "I'm probably doing the same," said Marie later, on a telephone call with her friend William. "Of course you are, honey," William said. They both laughed. "So, what am I not seeing?" asked Marie. "Ooooh," sighed William, "it's the scary parts. You have to talk about your relationship! But words can be a gift," he said, "if we're willing to be honest." So, Marie reached out to Michele, asking if the story had upset her, and if so, could they talk. *I've valued reconnecting with you over the past two years*, wrote Marie, *and would be sad to lose your friendship*. Michele's response contained two sentences only: *I'd be willing to talk with you in person. For many reasons, I won't be able to commit until after June sixteenth*. Alright then, thought Marie, I guess the story did upset her, and she forwarded Michele's response to Monica and William. *That's cold*, they wrote, or some variation. Marie thought it punishing, like Michele could be. But she took a deep breath and thanked Michele for her response. *June is fine*, she wrote, *though I am moving, so it will need to be before the twentieth*.

Inevitably, Marie remembered some of their stories. The time they stayed together at the Venice Beach Cotel—not quite a hostel, definitely not a hotel. They splurged on a private room and pushed their single beds together, laughing about the postcard collage of whitelady-bikini pictures that hung in the shared bathroom, and the single drink ticket they received at check-in for a vodka and orange juice ladled from a big plastic tub in the otherwise BYOB bar. The women liked being at the Cotel together, bragging about their adventures to the other MFA students (yes, this was during a residency) who were staying in more conventional, more expensive, hotels. There was the road trip to a feminist art conference in Idaho, hoping to see a Guerrilla Girl, but not calculating the time change, so they arrived an hour too late but with new sunglasses and truck stop caps and a silver mudflap decal of a sexy sitting girl taped to the back window of Marie's red truck. One time Marie reassured Michele that she absolutely was not narcissistic, no matter what her now-ex said. Many times, Marie got drunk and leaned all over Michele, and there was the time Marie met one of Michele's new boyfriends, whose most pronounced quality, as much as Marie could tell, was that he liked to have sex in public. That night, walking back to the car after a somewhat tedious dinner, he began calling Michele "Princess" in a teasing tone. "Stop it," said Michele, but he mock-bowed instead. "Princess," he said. "Does princess want a foot rub? Can I rub anything else?" Michele play-slapped him, and the new boyfriend asked Marie if her dad called her princess as well. Marie shook her head and Michele sighed. "I told him about fighting with Kristen in kindergarten over who was the real princess since both of our fathers called us by that name." "That's funny," said Marie, noting she'd never heard that story. "I never wanted to be a princess." "Of course you didn't," said Michele, "you'd be a horrible princess." The boyfriend laughed.

It was May and Marie decided there was an 80% chance that the June conversation with Michele wouldn't happen. "She'll chicken out," Marie said to Monica, "because she's actually legitimately afraid." "Of what," asked Monica, but Marie wasn't sure. "Maybe of losing her narrative or not controlling how she's perceived, maybe of being seen or feeling vulnerable, maybe of being right or wrong, of not being the Dom anymore, maybe of her own anger. Or maybe she's not afraid," continued Marie, "but simply pissed and hurt and has decided I'm not worth it. Maybe," said Marie, "I'm talking about myself," and she imagined a snake creating an ouroboros. "I don't think so," said Monica, "but you know what—you should write another fucking story."

Seems like a bad idea, thought Marie, for so many reasons. Seems like a good time to reconsider why, and for whom, we write. Seems there's no final answer to any big question, and why would we want one. Seems I'm reading an old friend as if the library is open on *RuPaul's Drag Race*, but she won't have a chance to grab the mic. Seems she could, maybe should, call me out, if she wants to. She's a writer, and here I am—reading myself, too. Listen, Michele, if you're there: you were my friend; this is my story. My experience of writing is also an experience of you, and writing is a performance that amplifies and flattens. You know this; you're a writer. I wanted to witness what I felt, all that learning and laughing. I'm not sorry for our friendship. Or for writing Marie; she's my friend, too.

Came. Coming. Can. Could. Marie learned the difference between permission and ability from the game "Mother May I," and the delight of the person playing Mother when, in response to the inevitable slip of *Mother can I*, Mother gets to say: *Sure, you can, but that doesn't mean you may.*

"To Michele," Marie said, as she opened her email. She had a scheduling conflict and wondered if they could change their meeting to either earlier that same day or anytime the next. There was a bit of back and forth about dates and times before Michele wrote that she'd given it more thought and decided she wasn't interested in meeting up. *I don't know if there will be a time, but it's not now.* Marie closed Michele's message, leaned back and looked at the corner, where wall met ceiling. If this were a game of chicken, thought Marie, Michele jumped first. "That's that then," said Marie to the screen. "Done." A small stream of sadness snuck in. Marie reopened Michele's message and forwarded it to Monica: *I was right*, she wrote, *oh well.* Marie shifted in her chair, looked at the oak tree outside her window. She thought of another writer she'd recently listened to at a city library event. He was queer, Moroccan, and his coming out had caused a big scandal in his community, as did his writing, making his mother's life more difficult by fueling the neighborhood gossip. For economies that run on reputations, gossip is gold. It took him, he said, three years to understand the tangible truth of his mother's experience, that his writing, in real ways, hurt her. He needed to understand this, he said. And still he wrote. Marie sighed and forwarded Michele's message to William. *I guess she couldn't show up*, wrote Marie. She re-closed Michele's message and stretched.

She felt lighter. It was Sunday evening. She needed to take out the kitchen trash.

An avocado from the neighbor's tree lay in the yard. Marie threw it over the fence, into the alley where she heard it land with a thud, followed by a scurrying sound. The movement triggered another neighbor's motion light, and when she opened the gate, she saw a raccoon. The creature stared as Marie felt a momentary panic, a freeze-frame of not knowing how, or if, to move. But the raccoon knew; they turned to grab the avocado and began to eat. Marie released her breath, opened the trash can, tossed the grey bag inside. There are times for secrecy, she thought, and times for curiosity. Times to wear the disguise, and times to hang the writing hat on a hook in the closet. That's what she wanted to say to Michele, but probably never would. In the night, the faint edge of a waxing moon shone in an otherwise clear sky. "Thank you," she said to the raccoon, and closed the gate.

"Endings are generally resisted," Monica said. It was the middle of the afternoon, several months later, and Monica and Marie were drinking lemonade at an outdoor café in the small Southern city where Monica now lived, having recently acquired a tenure-track position as a professor of creative writing. The women were discussing writing and friendships. "There are," said Monica, "friends for a reason, friends for a season, and friends for a lifetime. I read that," she grinned, "maybe on a greeting card." Marie laughed. "It's cheesy," admitted Monica, "but if the season has shifted or the reason has ended, I will cut that friendship off." Monica made a quick slicing gesture in the air. "Let that which was good stay good," she smiled, "otherwise, you invite discord, contempt, resentment." "Which can," said Marie, "change everything that came before." Monica nodded. "A reason," she said, "to write about it." Marie laughed and shook her head. "Okay then, let me tell you a story:

"In time, as the two women nurtured internal visions, their friendship, inevitably it seemed, came to an end."

About the Author

Teresa Carmody (she/they) is a writer of fiction, creative nonfiction, inter-arts collaborations, and hybrid forms. Her books include *The Reconception of Marie* (2020), *Maison Femme: a fiction* (2015), and *Requiem* (2005). Their writing has appeared in *LitHub, Los Angeles Review of Books, Michigan Quarterly Review, WaterStone Review, Lifework*, and elsewhere. A co-founding director of Les Figues Press in Los Angeles, Carmody currently lives in Omaha and teaches in the Writer's Workshop and low-residency MFA in Creative Writing Program at University of Nebraska Omaha.

Acknowledgments

To my mother, Janice Carmody, for everything. To my siblings and my mother's siblings, who have supported me in big and small ways. Thank you to Q. Catherina, Ms. Jane, and all my ascended ancestors: physical, intellectual, spiritual.

To my friends and family, many of whom read drafts of this work and who have encouraged me while writing: Prageeta Sharma, Ryan Rivas, Vidhu Aggarwal, Lucy Corin, Chad Anderson, Rajesh Reddy, Danielle Lopez, Pam Ore, Coco Owen, Christine Myers, Brandi Homan, Anna Joy Springer, Mona Awad, Bridge Kennedy, Connie Samaras, Karen Carmody, Mildred Bayra, Karen Daley, Sherise Reeves, Monica Morris, Chesya Burke, Alisha Rodriguez, Alyssa Brillinger, Maude Place, Fergus Place, Janice Lee, Julian Smith-Newman, Yolanda Pourciau, Urayoán Noel, Amanda Annis, derek beaulieu, Lindsey Drager, and Mike Stussy. Thank you.

To my professors at University of Denver: Selah Saterstrom, Dr. Tayana Hardin, Laird Hunt, Brian Kiteley, and Bin Ramke. Thank you for your insight, encouragement, and example. And to Lou Florez and Dorothea Lasky for leading that writing workshop under a full Worm moon.

To my animal companions: Gretel, Mary Corey, and Lucas Francisco Miguel de la Fabulosa.

To my colleagues and students at University of Nebraska Omaha. And to my students and colleagues at Stetson University, especially to those in the MFA of the Americas low-residency program.

Thank you to Ryan Rivas and Michael Wheaton. This book wouldn't exist without you and is better for your attention, care, and brilliance.

Thank you to those I have learned from and worked alongside to create events and organizations that envision a more just and equitable world, and that celebrate all kinds of art, artists, and lovers.

•

Earlier versions of several stories were published in the following journals; I would like to thank the editors for their support.

"Angela Writes Herself a Wife" was published as "Almost Worthy of Such a Wife" in *Juked*, 2014.

"William and His Women Friends" was published in The *Collagist*, and selected by *Longform*, as "Fiction Pick of the Week," 2016.

"A New Writing Friend" was published in *The Collagist*, 2016.

"Carol Krusen Helps a Friend" was published in *The Collagist*, 2017.

A version of "How Frederick Hides to See" was published as "Hide and See" in a limited-edition chapbook by No Press, Canada, 2018.

"A Healthy Interest in the Lives of Others" (parts I and II) were published in *Big Fiction*, 2019. The story was written using language gathered during a panel at Open Press 2016, with contributions by Anonymous, K. Bradford, Dale Enggass, Brenda Iijima, Rosa Quesada, Lara Schoorl, Anna Joy Springer, Stephen van Dyck, Laura Woltag, and many others who preferred not to share their names.

A version of "Marie Studies the Fine Art of Release" was published as "Give Away" in *St. Petersburg Review*, 2019.

"Trash Talk" was published in *Western Humanities Review,* 2019.

"Work Friends, or the Elements of Fiction Make a Story Go Go," selected by contest judge Lucy Ives as the "2024 Prose Contest Runner-Up," and published in *Fugue 65*.

— also from Autofocus Books —

Duplex — Mike Nagel

XO — Sara Rauch

Until It Feels Right — Emily Costa

Cleave — Holly Pelesky

Nextdoor in Colonialtown — Ryan Rivas

Too Much Tongue — Adrienne Marie Barrios & Leigh Chadwick

Picture Window — Danny Caine

the nature machine! — Tyler Gillespie

A Kind of In-Between — Aaron Burch

How to Write a Novel: An Anthology of 20 Craft Essays About Writing, None of Which Ever Mention Writing — ed. Aaron Burch

Hiraeth — Mistie R. Watkins

That Spell — Tate N. Oquendo

My Modest Blindness — Russell Brakefield

A Calendar Is A Snakeskin — Kristine Langley Mahler

Culdesac — Mike Nagel

Razed by TV Sets — Jason McCall

In the Away Time — Kristen E. Nelson

The Body Is A Temporary Gathering Place — Andrew Bertaina

Daughterhood — Emily Adrian

Leave: A Postpartum Account — Shayne Terry

Yes I Am Human I Know You Were Wondering — Erin Dorney